Shelby's hair was dirty and tangled around her face.

Smudges of dirt were on almost every inch of exposed skin, and what wasn't filthy was marred with scratches and bruises.

Jed couldn't imagine anyone looking more beautiful than she did right now.

And he couldn't stop himself from touching her. He cupped the back of her head and pulled her toward him. The moment their lips met, his tongue thrust inside for a raw, heated kiss, and she melted against him.

"Shelby..." He broke away, breathing hard. "I swear, if you ever pull a stunt like this again, I'll keep you tied to the bed for the rest of your life."

The Shelby of the past would have been angered by his arrogance. The new Shelby merely smiled. "And the same goes for you, darling.... Now, can we get out of here...?"

Dear Reader,

There's a nip in the air, now that fall is here, so why not curl up with a good book to keep warm? We've got six of them this month, right here in Silhouette Intimate Moments. Take Modean Moon's *From This Day Forward*, for example. This Intimate Moments Extra title is a deeply emotional look at the break-up—and makeup—of a marriage. Your heart will ache along with heroine Ginnie Kendrick's when she thinks she's lost Neil forever, and your heart will soar along with hers, too, when at last she gets him back again.

The rest of the month is terrific, too. Jo Leigh is back with *Everyday Hero*. Who can resist a bad boy like T. J. Russo? Not Kate Dugan, that's for sure! Then there's Linda Randall Wisdom's *No More Mister Nice Guy*. Jed Hawkins is definitely tough, but even a tough guy has a heart—as Shelby Carlisle can testify by the end of this compelling novel. Suzanne Brockmann's TALL, DARK AND DANGEROUS miniseries continues with *Forever Blue*, about Lucy Tait and Blue McCoy, a hero as true blue as his name. Welcome Audra Adams to the line with *Mommy's Hero*, and watch as the world's cutest twin girls win over the recluse next door. Okay, their mom has something to do with his change of heart, too. Finally, greet our newest author, Roberta Tobeck. She's part of our WOMEN TO WATCH new author promotion, and once you've read *Under Cover of the Night*, you'll know why we're so keen on her.

Enjoy—and come back next month for six more top-notch novels of romance the Intimate Moments way.

Leslie Wainger,
Senior Editor and Editorial Coordinator

Please address questions and book requests to:
Silhouette Reader Service
U.S.: 3010 Walden Ave., P.O. Box 1325, Buffalo, NY 14269
Canadian: P.O. Box 609, Fort Erie, Ont. L2A 5X3

NO MORE MISTER NICE GUY

LINDA RANDALL WISDOM

Published by Silhouette Books

America's Publisher of Contemporary Romance

SILHOUETTE BOOKS

ISBN 0-373-07741-6

NO MORE MISTER NICE GUY

LINDA RANDALL WISDOM

first sold to Silhouette Books on her wedding anniversary in 1979 and hasn't stopped since! She loves looking for the unusual when she comes up with an idea, and only hopes her readers enjoy reading her stories as much as she enjoys writing them.

A native Californian, she is married and has two dogs, five parrots and a tortoise, so life is never boring—or quiet—in the Wisdom household. When she isn't writing, she enjoys going to the movies, reading, making jewelry and fabric painting.

Many thanks to Adrian Paul, a.k.a. Duncan MacLeod of the Clan MacLeod, the Highlander, for giving romance writers a wonderful hero to draw upon. As far as many of us are concerned, Duncan is the Only One.

Prologue

Jed had to know if her soul was as fiery as her hair.

With the crystal tumbler of whiskey, neat, in one hand, he stood by a doorway where he could be out of the way and still easily watch her dazzle everyone around her.

She stood across the room looking like a brilliant flame, beckoning him to her side. There was only one problem. Flames could burn a person, and he wasn't into pain. Still, this was one time when the pain might be worth it.

It wasn't just her porcelain skin or flame red hair streaked with strands of rich gold, copper, bronze and blond. It wasn't even the black, strapless, sequined gown that hugged every curve.

It was the incredible energy that seemed to flow all around her body. She stood there looking like every man's fantasy come vividly to life. Judging by the expressions on the faces of the men in her vicinity, Jed doubted he was the only one who saw her that way. Who visualized her in his bed.

Jed didn't need to ask the identity of the lady with the fiery hair. He already knew her name and her vital statistics.

But dry statistics weren't the same as the real thing. For Jed, studying his subject in the flesh was much more enjoyable than reading facts and figures on a sheet of paper. Especially when the subject was as lovely as this one.

Shelby Elizabeth Carlisle. A natural redhead, with eyes the color of multifaceted emeralds. Five feet seven inches, with measurements worthy of a woman who worked out with a personal trainer four times a week. Twenty-nine years old and known for her fashion sense, she was well traveled, articulate, intelligent and pampered to within an inch of her life. He knew she was a born and bred Californian who made her home in one of the more refined Los Angeles suburbs and shunned the beach for the glitzy boutiques on Rodeo Drive and had even somehow turned her love for shopping into a business.

Not the kind of woman Jed normally associated with. He generally liked ones who knew the score. He could sense that while Shelby looked the part of the jaded jet-setter, she didn't play the game. He'd already heard about the past men in her life. He was surprised to learn she always remained good friends with them, even after the relationship was over. He wasn't sure he could be so generous as to give her up graciously.

She was dangerous. He sensed it.

But that was all right. He was dangerous, too.

Jed ambled over to the small group surrounding Shelby, never once taking his eyes off her glittering form. He didn't miss the way her body stiffened for just a second as she glanced over her shoulder and noticed him. For a brief moment, flames flared in her eyes. He didn't smile in satisfaction. He wanted her kept off guard.

Beware, old friend, she's the boss's daughter, his common sense warned him. *Not a good idea to seduce her.*

Many times Jed listened to his common sense. It had saved his life more than once over the years. This was one time he ignored that voice.

"Miss Carlisle," he murmured, nodding in her direction.

Lips colored a warm glossy red curved upward in a welcoming smile that spread to her eyes. "You must be Jed Hawkins. My father mentioned you were working stateside now." She held out her hand. "Pleased to meet you."

He noticed that the emerald solitaire winking on her ring finger matched her eyes exactly. The sultry fragrance emanating from her skin teased his senses in all the right ways.

"I understand you've recently returned from Monte Carlo. Did you enjoy your stay?" he asked smoothly, holding her hand just long enough for his message to get through. *I'm attracted to you and you're attracted to me. What shall we do about it?*

"It's always lovely this time of year, although I usually prefer somewhere quieter," she replied. "But it was nice to get together with old friends."

"Shelby in a quiet place?" one of the men hooted. "Honey, anyone who looks like you deserves bright lights and parties. Not some of those off-the-track hellholes you like to choose for your getaways."

The man stepped back the moment Shelby's cool glance settled on him. "You may prefer the parties, Frasier, but there are times when peace and quiet allow a person to think. Although I realize that isn't one of your strong points. Thinking, that is."

"I just meant . . ." He faltered.

"Yes, I'm sure you did."

Jed hid his smile. So the lady could bite back. Good. The idea of her in a black negligee teased his mind. Followed by the mental picture of her wearing nothing.

He blamed his mental wanderings on a too-long-celibate life. His work didn't allow for long-term relationships, which was just fine with him.

Shelby raised her chin. Her delicate eyebrow arched upward as if she could read his mind.

"Have you met the others, Mr. Hawkins?" She quickly made introductions.

Jed nodded at each one. It wasn't difficult to notice that the men didn't appreciate his intrusion into their group and the few women there appeared to feel exactly the opposite. He ignored them all.

"Seems your father has pulled out all the stops in his effort to welcome you home," he commented, looking around the large ballroom filled with people dressed in tuxedos and formal gowns.

Hothouse flowers in fragile vases had been placed everywhere and waiters circulated with trays holding champagne-filled goblets or various tidbits to tempt the palate. Jed knew an orchestra would be providing dance music later. He turned back to find Shelby's gaze on him. He quickly discovered she wasn't as easy to read as he thought she would be. Jed always did enjoy a challenge.

All Shelby knew about Jed Hawkins was what her father had told her. One thing he had mentioned was that the man could prove dangerous to her peace of mind.

She had never known for sure what Jed Hawkins did. Stories that circulated about him gave him credit for everything, including the ability to walk on water. He traveled a great deal for Warren Carlisle's import/export firm and had been out of the country for the past four years at one of the overseas offices. Her father often referred to him as the Hawk.

"Just remember he didn't come by that name lightly," he had warned her that afternoon. "The man is lethal when it comes to women. He's broken more than his share of hearts along the way."

"Ah, but I'm your daughter," she had said lightly. "And everyone knows that trifling with Warren Carlisle's daughter is tantamount to a very painful death. Besides, I absolutely refuse to allow my heart to be broken."

She remembered now that Warren hadn't smiled back. "Jed wouldn't worry about that," he'd said. When she'd asked him why he'd invited Jed at all, her father had given her a cryptic response about the Hawk needing to be around civilized people again. Then he'd swiftly changed the subject.

Shelby hadn't given another thought to her father's second-in-command until now.

Suddenly she understood why Warren had warned her about the man.

Jed Hawkins was aptly named. She was certain his piercing gaze saw past her dress to the black, sheer lingerie she had chosen to wear. He looked at her as if he was a bird of prey and she was an unsuspecting jackrabbit.

He was devastating in the formal black tuxedo with the snowy white shirt highlighting his sun-darkened skin. Raven black hair was tied back in a renegade's ponytail. His face might not have been considered conventionally good-looking, but the intensity in his expression captured every woman's attention. He was six feet but appeared even taller thanks to an erect bearing; the animal grace in his movements prompted a woman to think of other ways that same agility might be displayed. Eyes the deep gray of storm clouds watched her intently. His voice was like rich dark velvet that seduced and beguiled. She already felt the strong magnetic pull of his personality.

She resisted the urge to smile. Little did he know that the last thing she would even consider was becoming another notch on his bedpost.

A small voice inside her told her that getting to know this man would greatly change her life.

Chapter 1

"**Y**ou slime! I cannot believe you are telling me this *now!*"

Jed's idea of bliss was the quiet time after making love with Shelby. With all the traveling he did for Warren, their time together was limited, and by mutual consent they spent most of it in bed. For a man whose idea of commitment was being with the same woman more than three months, the past eighteen months had come as a surprise to him. During that time, he had never once found himself bored or thinking it was time to buy her something pretty and move on. She had always taken his news of yet another trip with grace and a warm smile, and he could always count on an equally warm welcome back. It didn't appear she was taking the news as well this time.

He raised himself up on his elbow, the sheet slipping down to drape over his bare hip. When he'd broken the news about his early morning flight, he hadn't expected this kind of reaction.

"Hawkins, your timing absolutely stinks. It's bad enough you're doing this to me again, but to do it right after we've made love is despicable." Shelby seemed to snarl the words as she leapt out of bed and snatched her bra from the carpet. Her head whipped from right to left as she searched the room for the matching bikini underwear. She hopped on one foot as she climbed into them, then wrapped her bra around her chest. In her hurry, she left one hook undone.

Jed released a silent sigh of regret as he watched her cover up what he so much enjoyed looking at. Considering her mood, he decided the best thing to do was take the logical approach. Appear quiet and rational, and she'd understand why he hadn't wanted to break the news earlier of his leaving the next morning and thereby ruin their evening together.

"Shelby, you know very well my job has always required a great deal of traveling," he began.

Her eyes blazed brilliant green fire as she faced him. One hand crushed a tangerine silk T-shirt at her side. "With all the traveling you do, people would think you're the only capable person in the company," she stated coldly. "I can't believe you are so indispensable that you have to do all the traveling you're asked to do. There are others who are just as capable."

Jed mentally compared his capabilities with some of the others and instantly dismissed them. It wasn't conceit. He merely knew what he could do and what they could. He always won hands down.

"Not exactly." He didn't move as he watched her drop the top over her head and pull on matching silk trousers. Her movements were jerky, filled with anger as she tucked her shirt inside the waistband. He was amazed at this new side of Shelby. Until now she'd never displayed any form of temper in front of him. He'd thought she was one of the calmest women he'd ever known. This other side of her was proving to be fascinating. And arousing.

Shelby looked up and didn't miss the lambent glow in his eyes or his body's response. If anything, she looked angrier than she had before.

"You pig," she cried. "All you can think about is sex." She lifted her arm as if she would strike him. Where it would hurt the most. And she wasn't aiming at his ego.

Jed figured only his lightning-quick reflexes kept him from receiving a painful blow. He sat back against the headboard. "Are you going to tell me exactly why you're so angry with me?" he asked in his most reasonable voice.

Shelby shot him a look guaranteed to melt him into a tiny puddle. She stalked out of the room and came back carrying her purse. She wrenched her brush out of it and faced the dresser mirror, brushing her hair with furious strokes. When she finished, the tousled waves hung sleekly past her shoulders. Afterward, she carefully applied lipstick. Jed didn't miss the slight trembling in her fingers.

By the time she turned around, any sign of turmoil was erased from her expression and she almost looked serene. Yet he doubted this conversation would be anything close to serene.

"How long have we known each other, Jed?" she asked in a soft, controlled voice.

"Eighteen months, two weeks, four days," he said without hesitation.

A brief smile curved her lips at his literal answer. She picked up her pendant and slipped it around her neck. The heart-shaped, deep blue topaz swung down between her breasts. She picked up matching earrings and fastened them in her ears before sliding on her ring. "And how often have you been gone during those eighteen months, two weeks and four days?"

Jed frowned. He didn't like the direction this conversation was taking. "I believe six or seven times."

Shelby's smile held a tinge of sorrow. "Six or seven times? Give me a break, Jed. Your brain is better than any computer at storing information." She reached inside her purse and pulled out a small appointment book. She leafed through it.

"We knew each other exactly five days when you took your first trip. You were gone for two months," she told him. "Your second trip was three weeks after you returned that first time. Next time, you were gone for seven weeks. At last count, you have been absent a total of thirteen months, three weeks and one day during the eighteen months we've known each other."

She held her hand up to ward off any argument on his part. "I understand your work is important to you. I wouldn't dream of interfering with it. After all, my father did a lot of traveling when I was growing up. My mother tried to help me understand when he wasn't there for my birthday or for Christmas, but I never minded then. When it hurt for me were the times he wasn't there for their wedding anniversary or my mother's birthday.'' Shelby kept her gaze squarely on his face, but she didn't bother to hide the pain in her eyes. ''I don't want to have to hide the hurt the way my mother did. I can't go through this anymore.''

Jed felt his facial muscles tighten as he realized what was coming next.

''It's well known you don't believe in commitment,'' she said. ''And lately, I've decided that's something I want to add to my life. I want a relationship. I realize you aren't looking for one, so I feel it's best if we don't see each other anymore.''

He sat up now. ''You decided to drop this on me *after* we made love?''

''Don't you mean after we had sex? Jed, you are an incredible lover, and if I thought you had a heart, I would dearly love to fall in love with you. But why should I allow myself to have my heart broken by someone who doesn't truly deserve me?'' she asked in a voice so level he felt a slight simmering in his blood. ''And don't give me that nonsense about telling you the news afterward. Just remember it wasn't until after you got me into bed that you decided to let it slip you had a six a.m. flight to catch.''

''This is something we need to discuss further,'' Jed said in an equally level voice.

''That's nice. Personally, I don't think there's anything more to discuss.'' Shelby tucked her lipstick into her purse and picked up the leather bag.

He felt a trickle of unease travel up his back. "Where are you going?" he asked, even though he already had a good idea what her reply would be.

"Home." She draped the purse's strap over her shoulder. "Don't worry about getting up. I can have Lucas call a cab for me." She referred to the guard on duty in the apartment building's lobby.

Jed was out of bed and across the room in a flash. Shelby had barely reached the doorway before he was there, blocking it. Now the fury in his gaze was taking over his body. His muscles looked so tight she was surprised they didn't snap.

"If you are so insistent on going home now, I will drive you," he stated. "But I feel it's only right you allow me my say before you leave."

She didn't bat an eyelash. "Have the courtesy not to treat me like a three-year-old having a tantrum, Jed. I can make it home on my own."

"Then at least have the courtesy to hear me out." His facial muscles pulsed as he paused before saying a word he rarely used. "Please."

Shelby nodded silently and turned around.

No less imposing even when nude, Jed waited until Shelby walked over to the bed and sat on the end. She looked up at him with the same bland expression she would have given a stranger.

Jed had to give her credit—she was hiding her feelings very well. If he didn't know her as intimately as he did, he wouldn't have guessed just how much she was hurting inside. And that hurt him.

But there was nothing he could do about that.

"You knew from the beginning how demanding my job is," he began. "I have always done a great deal of traveling for Carlisle Imports, and coming out here seemed to mean more travel instead of less. Because of my expertise in certain matters, someone else cannot just step into my shoes at the last minute."

"Not to mention you really wouldn't *want* anyone to step into your shoes, would you?" she asked softly. For a moment, bitter pain was reflected in her eyes. "After all, there might be someone out there who's better than you, and you'd hate that, wouldn't you? You know, from the very beginning I always felt as if you led two lives—one when you're here and one you lead when you're traveling...."

"If you're implying I have a woman in every port, you are very wrong." Danger laced his tone. "I haven't been with anyone from that first time I saw you. I haven't wanted anyone else."

"I'm not accusing you of having other women, Jed," Shelby said wearily. All of a sudden she felt very tired. "I don't think there's another man I know who is as honorable as you are. All I know is I feel it's time I have more. I deserve it. And I'm adult enough to know you aren't the man to give it to me."

He shifted uneasily. "I sent you flowers on your birthday and we celebrated as soon as I got back."

She waved her hand to indicate he wasn't truly listening to what she was saying. "I'm not talking about missed birthdays or Christmas or even Easter. I'm talking about knowing someone is there. When you're gone, I have no idea where you are. I can't reach you by telephone except by going through the office, and then it's only for extreme emergencies. The one time I did call you, I didn't hear back for days."

Jed thought about the time she referred to. His building manager had phoned with a question about his apartment. In the end, Jed had let him know Shelby was authorized to make any decisions in his absence. Jed had thought it would make things easier all the way around. He hadn't considered it a sign that he was counting on her as more than just a convenient bedmate when he was in town.

Funny, he never worried about Shelby when he was gone. He always felt sure she'd be there when he returned. Now she was telling him she wanted him out of her life. He'd be back to a lonely existence again. That was a prospect he wasn't looking forward to, although it would take a lot of torture for him to admit it.

As he studied her face he realized there was a great deal more than anger inside her. He also saw pain and resignation. He wondered what she would say if he told her it wasn't his fear of commitment but rather of eventual rejection that kept him from any long-term relationship. Still, if there was a woman he could see a future with, it was Shelby. He doubted she'd really want him for the long haul. No one else ever had. And Warren Carlisle, with his pedigree that could be traced back to the *Mayflower,* wouldn't want a mongrel in his family.

"I'm sorry I have that early flight, but we can talk when I get back," he said at last.

She shook her head. "No more talk, Jed. It isn't going to make a difference. You can't, or won't, change, and I need more than you can offer." She stood up and walked toward the door.

This time he stepped aside. "This isn't over, Shelby," he informed her, following her through the darkened rooms until she reached the front door. "Not by a long shot."

The twisting in his gut tightened as he watched her pull his door key off her key ring and place it gently on the hall table.

"We will talk when I get back," Jed stated. "If I could put off this trip, I would, but it can't be done. I'm sorry, Shel."

She shook her head. As she opened the door and stepped into the lighted hallway, he couldn't help but notice the tears in her eyes.

"So am I, Jed. So am I," she whispered, closing the door behind her.

He simply stood there, stunned.

He'd had no idea she wanted a commitment. In all this time, she hadn't given him a hint about her feelings. He'd thought she was happy with the way things were, as he undeniably was. The missions were proving more nerve-racking each time, and sometimes the only thing that kept him going was the thought of seeing Shelby when he got back.

He thought of throwing on clothing and going downstairs after her, but instantly dismissed the idea. By the time he got down there, Lucas would have already put her in a taxi.

Jed walked back to the bedroom. The first thing he noticed was the scent of Shelby's perfume lingering in the air. He knew it was imprinted on his bed linens, as well as his senses.

He refused to believe she meant what she'd said.

"She's just irritated I'm leaving again," he told himself, pulling back the sheets with a ruthless sweep of his hand. His first notion was to strip the bed, then he changed his mind. He'd sleep better with her scent in his nostrils. "I'll send her flowers and arrange to meet her for dinner when I get back. Warren will help her understand."

As Jed climbed into bed, he knew it wasn't going to be easy. What do you do when you can't tell the woman you're involved with that you're actually a government agent and your traveling isn't for an import/export firm after all?

You told her the best story you could and hoped it would be enough.

"No." Shelby picked up the vase of roses and dropped them into the wastebasket, which wobbled from side to side with the weight of the vase. Luckily, it remained upright. She dusted off her hands and walked around the desk to sit in her chair.

Warren grimaced at the sight of the fragile crystal sitting in the wastebasket. "That is the sixth bouquet you've thrown away. Do you realize what those roses cost?"

She picked up her gold pen and began sorting through invoices. "Seven, but who's counting?"

Her father sat in the visitor's chair. Dressed in a navy suit with a crisp white shirt and navy-and-burgundy floral tie, he was a tribute to Shelby's excellent fashion sense. Shelby might have a wealthy father and a trust fund from her mother's family, but she still ran her own business—a personal shopping service. What had started out as shopping trips with friends to help them select new wardrobes had quickly evolved into a career as she assisted friends of friends with gift ideas and any shopping they didn't have the time or inclination to do. Even some of her trips overseas turned into shopping expeditions as she discovered items she knew some of her clients would want.

"I always felt you and Jed made the perfect couple." Warren picked up a paperweight on Shelby's desk and idly examined the delicate snowscape inside. "I've never met a man more devoted to someone the way that he is to you. I won't lie and say I didn't have high hopes for you two."

She didn't look up from her desk. "It won't work, Daddy. While you had those hopes, he didn't."

Warren went on as if she hadn't spoken. "Honey, Jed is a man with high principles. He's someone you can trust with your life. There are few men I would trust with my daughter the way I trust him."

Shelby glanced up. "Even if he's been doing the dirty deed with your darling daughter?" she asked with deliberate malice.

Warren winced.

She leaned forward and cooed, "Oh, but it probably bothers you thinking of your little girl having a sex life, doesn't it? After all, I'm supposed to remain a virgin until I'm married. Not hop into bed with Jed Hawkins. Sorry, Dad, these are the nineties."

"If your mother could hear you right now, she would wash your mouth out with soap. I don't want to hear any more about your sex life." He spoke slowly, as if the words pained him.

"Fine, because I have nothing more to say. Now, if you don't mind," she said, sitting back in her chair, "there will be no more mention of Jed Hawkins. You can just toddle on back to your office and do whatever you do there." She shook her head with disgust. "I swear, if I didn't know better I'd think you were spies with all your secrets."

Luckily, her head was bowed and she missed the swift look of shock that crossed his face before he masked his expression.

"You do realize Jed should be getting back in about four weeks?" he asked.

She didn't look up. "Good for him."

"You're not going to give him a chance, are you?"

Shelby put her pen down and tilted her head back. Today her lustrous hair was arranged in a Gibson, styled with soft tendrils curling down her cheeks. Her cream-colored blouse had a lace collar that added to her old-fashioned appearance. If it wasn't for the steel in her eyes, a man would think she was no more substantial than cotton candy. But Warren knew his daughter well. When she had that expression in her eyes, even a nuclear bomb wouldn't budge her.

"Give me one good reason why I should?" she invited.

"He's the best man you'll ever find."

Shelby didn't look away. "But will he be there for me when I truly need him? Or off on another trip?" She smiled when Warren remained silent. "No offense, Daddy, but you forget something. Jed enjoyed things as long as our relationship was kept open-ended. If I hadn't severed it when I did, he would have eventually. It's much better that I did it first. Now, if you don't mind, I would like to get these out in this afternoon's mail." She returned to her work.

Warren stood up. He thought sadly of the many secrets he had guarded over the years. How they had forced him to have another life separate from his family. He wanted to tell Shelby about the reasons behind Jed's travels, the danger the man was in every trip he took. At the same time, Warren wasn't sure it would make a difference. For all he knew, she might still decide it was better if she and Jed stayed apart.

Yet deep down Warren had the feeling that Jed wasn't going to let Shelby just walk out of his life.

"All right. Perhaps you'd care to join me for dinner tonight?" He started for the door.

"Daddy," she called after him. "Don't start thinking up any elaborate schemes for Jed's homecoming. Meredith asked me if I'd like to go up to her family's mountain cabin, and we'll be leaving around that time. We thought it would be a good time of year to get away from it all and commune with nature."

Warren bit back his curse. It appeared she knew him as well as he knew her. "How long will you be gone?"

"I don't know, but I'm sure you'll honor my request for privacy and not tell Jed where I've gone."

He swallowed another curse. "You know very well I wouldn't do that."

Shelby smiled. "Oh, yes, you would, you old faker. That's why I want your promise you won't say anything."

"All right, I promise." The words were torn from him with great reluctance.

"Thank you, and yes, I would love to have dinner with you this evening. I can be ready at seven."

Warren opened her office door and started out, then stopped and turned. "You may claim you're over the man, but I think if you'd listen to your heart, you'd find out differently."

"If I'd listened to my heart in the first place, I would have known better than to get involved with someone like him," she said softly.

After Warren left, Shelby felt safe enough to collapse back in her chair. The tension of holding herself together was wearing on her nerves. Right now she felt like a piece of overcooked spaghetti.

She didn't want to admit she still cried herself to sleep almost every night. She didn't want to admit she had saved a rose from every bouquet that arrived and pressed it in a book. She didn't want to admit she was already in love with Jed. Admitting it made it true, and she couldn't handle that kind of truth right now.

She vowed that, no matter what, she would get on with her life. Even if the life she would be leading from now on would be nothing more than a bleak existence.

Chapter 2

"This is what I call heaven, even if there aren't any decent men around to provide some lovely scenery." Meredith Ackerman gave a sigh as she relaxed in a chaise lounge on the wraparound porch. She stretched out legs that seemed to go on forever. Her brief white shorts and white, midriff-baring halter top showed off her deep golden tan. Even if there weren't any men around, she believed in dressing to attract. She twisted her feet one way, then the other to admire the pearly, rose-colored nail polish she'd used on her toenails. "I never thought I could enjoy peace and quiet, but I have to admit being here has recharged my batteries better than any of my stays at the spa." She thought for a moment. "Well, unless you include the time that Italian count was there," she mused.

"It's relaxing here because you're not worrying about rushing to your next aerobics class or making your facial appointment on time. Not to mention all your wondering about which man is available." Shelby was content to lay back with her eyes closed as the warm afternoon sun warmed her skin. "I am so glad you suggested we come up here. I really needed this."

Until they had arrived at the cabin ten days ago, she hadn't realized how badly she needed this getaway. Shelby had left the phones to Clara, who would explain Ms. Carlisle was out of town and would schedule appointments for Shelby's return. She enjoyed having a career that gave her the freedom to take time off when she wished. Plus, she always tended to snoop around shops wherever she went in case she happened to find just the right item she knew a client would appreciate.

Even though she had ordered herself not to think about Jed, it proved to be easier said than done. Especially when she knew he should have returned about a week ago. She wondered if Meredith's timing was deliberate. Knowing her friend, it was. After all, Shelby had whisked her away to that desert spa when Meredith's latest love had left her for a cosmetics clerk. To date, Meredith hadn't stepped one foot inside that department store even though it had been one of her favorites.

"Oh, come on, Shelby. Do you honestly think coming up here will allow you to forget about Jed?" Meredith asked.

Shelby hid her grimace of dismay. There were times when she wondered if her friend read minds. "Jed who?" she asked innocently.

Meredith rolled her eyes. "Oh, puleeze! You know very well I'm talking about one of the sexiest men these eyes have seen in a long time. I cannot believe you think you can just say he's out of your life like that—" she snapped her fingers "—and he'll meekly go his own way. No tantrum, no screaming on your part. You have great restraint, my dear."

"You think he's so great? He's yours," Shelby offered. "In fact, you have my blessing, my child. Go for it."

"I wish it was that easy." Meredith sat up on the chaise and crossed her legs in the lotus position. Since she'd started yoga classes, she chose to show off her flexibility any chance she had. "There's just one problem. The man only has eyes for you. It doesn't take much to see that he is wrapped around your little finger."

Shelby picked up her glass of iced tea. "If he was wrapped around my little finger, he wouldn't have gone on this last trip."

"How dare the man!" her friend drawled. "To think he would fly off on business when he could be home catering to your every whim! The man should be shot!" she declared, with her usual dramatic flair.

Shelby sat up and swung her legs around so she could better see her friend. "Not cute, Mer." She used the nickname she'd given her the first day they'd met, back in kindergarten. "Ever since I can remember, my father has had to travel for his business. It seems owning an import/export firm means you're not allowed to stay home a lot. He cut back on his traveling for a while after Mom's death, but soon he was gone more than he was home." She frowned as she thought about those empty years. "I'm officially over thirty. I'm finding out I need more."

"Aren't we all?" Meredith said. When Shelby shot her a quelling glare, she quickly raised her hands in surrender. "All right, I'll behave, but do you see me complaining about my biological clock ticking? Still, it might have something to do with my always hitting the snooze button on that little bugger."

"That's because you're always having to make up your mind between two or three men. I want just one."

"Meaning you want Jed Hawkins's ring on your third finger, left hand?" Meredith gave her friend a look filled with sympathy. "Oh, honey, from that first meeting you should have known he was not the commitment type. The sparks striking off the two of you might have been able to start a major forest fire, but that didn't mean he'd stay around to keep it going. That's why he enjoys all that travel. Didn't you tell me his apartment looks more like a hotel suite than a home? That alone says a lot about his personality." She reached across the space separating the two lounges and placed her hand on Shelby's arm. "I have an idea. The last thing we need is to sit here and turn maudlin with all this talk about men. Why don't we think about flying down to Cancun? Or even New York for some serious shopping. The best way to mend a broken heart is to spend lots of money. New clothes to go with that new look of yours." She stared at her friend. "You know, I still can't get used to your hair." She shook her head in disbelief. "Since high school you've only had trims."

Shelby appeared uncertain as she reached up and touched the tousled strands. Hair that had been a shimmering, fiery waterfall down her back now barely touched her neck. Today, it was pulled up into a short ponytail. She didn't want to think it was shorter than Jed's. Nor remember how he loved to comb his fingers through her hair as he made love to her. Just the thought of how it felt when he possessed her was enough to send shivers through her body.

"I decided it was time to get it cut short. Besides, it's easier to take care of," she argued.

"I have to admit the style is cute on you. It'll just take getting used to," Meredith continued. "That settles it. You need a new wardrobe to go with the new hair! Wouldn't a marathon shopping spree in the big city be fun? We could even take in a few shows."

"But I like the solitude here..." Shelby protested. Her words drifted off as she peered past Meredith's shoulder, her forehead furrowed.

"What's wrong?" Meredith twisted around, but saw only rows of trees and a boathouse down by the small lake. Since her father enjoyed fishing, a motorboat was kept in the boathouse year-round.

Shelby shook her head. "Nothing, I guess. Maybe it was just a reflection from the water. For a moment I could have sworn I saw someone among the trees on the other side of the lake."

"We see the occasional hikers, since there's a good trail not far from here, but they've never come too close," Meredith replied. "We've been lucky that no one's ever broken into the cabin in all these years. All right, if you want to stay here and vegetate, we'll turn into literal porch potatoes. I just hope when we get back you'll remember to withstand Jed's lethal charm when he comes after you. And he will. I can't imagine he's going to let you go that easily."

"I made Daddy promise not to tell him where I was, and one thing he does is keep his promises. Besides, he knows what would happen to him if he did tell Jed. As for Jed, why would he bother to waste his time coming after a woman who basically dumped him?" Shelby hitched up her shorts to gain maximum tanning rays on her legs. "He has too much pride for that. He'll just go on and find someone new." She ignored the pang deep in her stomach at the idea of Jed with another woman.

Meredith's eyes widened as the truth hit her like a ton of bricks. "Oh, Shel, you're in love with him, aren't you?"

She nodded. "Unfortunately."

Her friend shook her head. "If love makes a body that miserable, I'm better off falling in and out of love at the drop of a hat. At least I'm not risking anything."

"Yes, but you don't feel you're truly alive until you've experienced the real thing," Shelby whispered.

"Now I *know* I'll pass on that experience, thank you very much. No offense, Shel, but the man is so controlled it's as if he doesn't have a nerve in his body. Although, there must be one good nerve or you wouldn't still be hung up on him." She shot her friend a sly look, then continued, "But no matter how much heat he generates with a single glance, it's as if he holds something back."

Shelby nodded. "He holds back a good part of himself. And yes, he keeps himself very controlled. Yet sometimes I would get this very brief glimpse of something deep down and I'd always hope and pray I'd see more of that hidden part of him." She looked thoughtful. "I don't feel I was being greedy in wanting all of him."

"True. Not when you're talking about someone who looks like him." Meredith affected a delicious shudder. "Those gorgeous eyes of his seem to look at a woman and know all her secrets."

"While making sure not to give away any of his own," Shelby murmured, feeling a familiar pain in the region of her heart. She suddenly straightened. "You know what I would like, Mer?" She didn't bother waiting for a reply. "I would like to see Jed lose that icy control just once. I want him to turn into a wild man. You know the kind I mean—a primitive who throws me over his shoulder and carries me off to his cave to have his way with me."

Meredith chuckled. "Oh, right, the ice man will lose all that iron control of his and turn into the ultimate barbarian. You know very well that if Jed tried anything like that you'd fillet him with words."

Shelby dropped back against the chaise. "Maybe I would and maybe I wouldn't," she said softly. "I'd sure like the chance to find out."

When they went inside the cabin an hour later, Shelby couldn't stop herself from glancing over her shoulder toward the stand of trees near the lake. For a moment, she thought she saw something silver wink at her. She knew if she said anything to Meredith her friend would just scoff and say it was a gum wrapper on the ground. Shelby wasn't as certain it could be dismissed so easily.

She was just feeling paranoid, she told herself. After all, why would anyone want to watch them?

The ear-splitting sound of the alarm blared overhead as the front door of the cabin exploded inward. Shelby scrambled out of bed in time to see a figure rush along the dark hallway. Harsh orders were issued, strict commands that they stay quiet and not give any trouble if they wanted to stay alive.

"Who the hell are you?" Meredith shrieked just as Shelby ran out of her room. Shelby looked down the hall to see her friend struggling with a man. The sound of a hand striking skin was followed by Meredith's pain-filled cry. A thud was the last sound Shelby heard her make.

"Meredith!" she screamed, as the figure turned on her. "You son of a bitch!" She lashed out, punching and kicking with every ounce of energy in her body. Judging from his curses, she connected a few times. "Let me go!" When he covered her mouth with his hand, she wrenched her head back and let loose an ear-splitting scream.

Before Shelby could fight anymore, she found her hands painfully wrenched behind her back and tied with a piece of rough rope that chafed her wrists.

"Hey, girlie, you're a real pretty one. Not like that other broad," a raspy male voice breathed in her ear. "You got class. I can tell. Always wanted me a woman with class. I hear you classy ones are real hot in the sack. I can't wait to find out."

Shelby fought down the panic that desperately tried to claw its way free as she visualized her fate with this man. Along with the panic came nausea as foul breath coupled with even worse body odor attacked her senses. She thanked her stars she didn't vomit when a smelly cloth was jammed in her mouth and tied behind her head. When her legs collapsed and she fell to the floor, she was roughly dragged to her feet and pushed down the hallway. Shelby silently prayed that he wouldn't drag her back into her bedroom. Shelby's imagination ran wild with worst case scenarios as she stumbled when he pushed her again. As she was pulled past the open doorway to Meredith's room, where a bedside lamp glowed, she saw her friend lying on the floor. Shelby almost screamed when she saw blood forming a dark pool around her head.

Spots danced before Shelby's eyes as she felt her own body start to shut down.

"Now don't you think about passing out, cuz I sure don't intend to carry you," the man rasped in her ear. Suddenly, he shouted, "Andy, are you back downstairs yet to see what they got?"

"Yeah. And I found a coupla high-powered rifles, plenty of ammo and lots of food in the kitchen! I found a bunch of other stuff we can use. Uncle Eric's gonna be real happy with what we got here, Chris."

Shelby didn't want to hear names. She didn't want to know what the men looked like. She only wanted them to take whatever they wanted and leave her alone. The image of Meredith lying helpless in her bedroom filled Shelby with dread. She didn't want to think the worst about her friend's condition.

"Yeah, well, look what I found." The man called Chris pushed her so hard, she stumbled down the stairs.

Shelby was grateful she was wearing shorty pajamas instead of a revealing nightgown.

"Wow! She's really pretty!" The other man stood at the foot of the stairs and looked up.

Shelby's spirits sank even further as, in the light of the small lamp near the front door, she got a good look at the two men.

They could have been twins. Both had dark hair, greasy and dirty, hanging to their shoulders, and beards that looked moth-eaten. The ragged overalls they wore without shirts were as dirty as they themselves were, although their hiking boots looked expensive. She wondered where they had stolen them from.

"Uncle Eric's gonna be real happy we found someone pretty like her. The last one wasn't near as sexy as she is," her captor said as he pushed her toward the door. "Here, gorgeous, you better put these on, cuz we got a lotta walking to do and we wouldn't want you to hurt your feet, would we?" He pushed her against the wall and jammed a pair of leather loafers on her feet, then slid his callused fingers up her legs in a leisurely caress.

It wasn't until then that Shelby realized they intended to take her with them. She almost didn't notice they'd given her a pair of Meredith's shoes, which were a half size too small. Shelby fought the urge to kick him where it counted for daring to touch her this way.

She was so angry she started to tell them just what she thought of them, but with the gag in her mouth, her words were garbled. In a fit of temper, she kicked out at the man nearest her, but his leg must have been fashioned of pure oak. All she managed to do was hurt her toes and make him mad.

"Bitch!" he snarled, swinging back his hand.

Shelby was positive she saw stars when it connected with her cheek. She felt herself sliding down the wall as her legs collapsed under her. She thought her ears were ringing, too, until she realized it was the alarm still blaring away. So much for security systems keeping burglars out and bringing help immediately.

"Dammit, Chris, don't damage her or Uncle Eric'll have our hides!" the other man scolded, grabbing hold of Shelby's arm and pulling her upright. "C'mon. We gotta get out of here 'fore the cops show up."

Shelby was so dazed she was out the door and halfway across the yard before she realized it. As they alternately dragged and pushed her toward the woods, movies ran through her head—pictures of women kidnapped by mountain men who performed unspeakable acts on them. Tears pricked her eyelids and streamed down her cheeks, to gather in the stiff fabric bunched around her mouth. She barely managed to stay upright as she struggled up the hill.

"Don't worry, pretty girl," her captor whispered in her ear, pinching her breast. "If Uncle Eric don't want you, I do. I won't let you feel too lonely."

Shelby gritted her teeth against the obscene touch. She only wished her hands were free so she could show him what she thought of his suggestion. Her saner side told her it was just as well she couldn't.

The strong pull in her calves would have told her they were moving uphill even if she hadn't seen the faint outline of the mountain ahead as dawn approached. The men moved swiftly, with no regard for the fact that she had to take three steps to their one. As she forced her feet to move, she ordered herself to not even think about their destination.

If I get out of this in one piece I promise to tell Jed I want to be with him on whatever terms he sets, she prayed, already wincing with each step she took. *If he'll take me back, I'll do anything he wants. I'll go to the airport and smile and wave goodbye when he goes on his damn trips. Smile when he comes back. I won't even mention the words* relationship *or* commitment *to him. And please,* please *let someone find Meredith and let her be all right.* Shelby was so afraid to think her friend might be dead. If she believed that, she would collapse in a pile of tears and never get up again. *And last of all, please let someone find me!*

Jed hadn't expected the mission to run over as long as it had. By rights, he should have been back a week ago. He blamed it on his thoughts of Shelby. Damn her for throwing a tantrum right before he left! Damn her for not responding to his flowers. Just plain damn her.

Feeling tired and out of sorts, he descended from the private jet. With the late hour, all he could think of was a long hot shower and a double whiskey. He hadn't shaved in the past three days, and while the jet offered a bedroom and bathroom with all the amenities, he had settled in one of the chairs and begun writing up his report. He wanted to hand it to Warren first thing in the morning. He also wanted to talk to the man about the rumors he had heard while over there. Rumors that one of their men was working for both sides.

A traitor in their midst could prove dangerous for the entire overseas operation. And that kind of danger meant people's lives were at stake. Jed wished he could have tracked the man down while he was over there. But he would talk to Warren, make plans and go back. He doubted Shelby would be too eager to see him, but he'd give it his damnedest before he left.

When he reached the gate, he was surprised to find his superior standing there. He hadn't expected to see Warren until the next morning. What first struck him was the look of anguish on his face and the grayish tint to his skin. The older man's pained expression sent warning bells clanging in Jed's brain.

"What's wrong, Warren?" he demanded, grasping his boss's arm. The man looked ready to collapse, and Jed hated to think what trauma had brought him to this condition. "What's happened?"

"It's Shelby," Warren said tightly.

Jed stiffened. "Has she been ill? In an accident? *Dammit, what?*" His grip tightened.

Warren winced. Jed relaxed his fingers but didn't step back.

"She's..." Warren took a deep breath. When he lifted his face, his eyes were shining with tears. This show of emotion scared Jed more than the man's ill appearance. In all the years he'd known Warren Carlisle he had never seen him close to tears. But it was when the older man continued in a broken voice that Jed's heart turned cold. "She's been kidnapped."

Before Jed could utter a word, Warren's face turned a sickly gray and he started to fall to the ground.

"We need some help over here!" Jed shouted, as he grasped Warren's shoulders and tried to keep him on his feet. A second later, as he listened to his boss's gasping, he gently lowered him to the ground. He looked up at one of the employees running toward them. "Call an ambulance!"

"Don't worry about me," Warren rasped. "You have to find Shelby for me. She's all that matters." He suddenly gasped again and grabbed his chest.

The doctor who came out to inform Jed of Warren's condition looked at him warily. "He's had a heart attack," the man said bluntly. "From what I've heard, he's been under a lot of pressure the past few hours, since he learned of his daughter's disappearance. He wants to see you, but you must keep him as calm as possible. He's very fragile right now and prime material for another attack. He can't afford any stress."

Jed nodded jerkily as he quickly advanced to the cardiac critical-care unit. Seeing a man he'd always thought of as invincible hooked up to machines was a shock.

When Jed entered the tiny room, Warren opened his eyes. His skin was still gray, his eyes bloodshot. "She's somewhere in the Angeles National Forest," he mumbled without preamble. "There's a sheriff's deputy up there you can contact—Rick Howard. He'll fill you in on what they know, but I can tell you that it's damned little."

"How did it happen?"

Warren slowly shook his head. "Shelby had gone up with Meredith to her parents' cabin. It has an excellent security system and they've never had any problems, so I had no reason to worry about her. The alarm is hooked up to the sheriff's station, but by the time they got out to the cabin they found Shelby gone and the place trashed. All the weapons were taken, along with food and small items that could be easily fenced."

"What happened to Meredith?" Jed asked.

Warren closed his eyes momentarily, as if the answer was painful. "She was found in her bedroom. Whoever broke in roughed her up, and she fell against her dresser, hitting her head and cutting it open. They say she'll be okay. She gained consciousness long enough to tell them that she thought there were two men and that they smelled horrible." He smiled faintly. "To Meredith, anyone who doesn't wear designer cologne smells terrible. She had no idea what happened to Shelby, but tracks up the mountain showed they took her with them."

Jed touched his boss's hand, careful to bypass the tubes hooked into him. "I'll find her, Warren," he vowed.

"I knew you would," he whispered. "I already told the sheriff's department to aid you in any way they can. You're the only one I trust, Jed."

"And when I find her, I'm going to kiss her until she can't breathe, and once she's out of breath, I'm going to throttle her," Jed murmured as he left the room in long, angry strides.

Warren smiled as he settled back against his pillows. "Just the thing I wanted to hear."

Jed felt as if he was running on automatic pilot. The moment he stepped out of the hospital he found his car near the entrance, courtesy of one of Warren's men, who had driven it over for him. The man handed him the keys.

"It's a good thing you came home tonight. If you hadn't, one of us would have called you in," the agent told Jed. "I swear the old man aged twenty years when he got the news about his daughter. He kept saying you were the only one who could find her. I topped off the gas tank and threw in a thermos of strong coffee. Here are directions to the sheriff's station and names of who to see there." He handed Jed a sheet of paper detailing everything he would need to know.

Jed tossed his carry-on bag into the passenger seat. "I'll take my cellular with me, although I can't guarantee you'll be able to reach me once I'm up the mountain."

The man nodded as he stepped back. Without another word, Jed jumped into his car and raced out of the parking lot. Watching him leave, the agent prayed no police car would try to stop him. He hated to think what would happen to any poor cop who tried to write the Hawk a ticket tonight.

Shelby couldn't remember ever feeling this tired. None of her aerobic classes or sessions with her personal trainer had prepared her for this trek up the mountain. She was positive her lungs were ready to burst, while the two men were barely breathing fast. They had continued walking for a few hours, then stopped for a quick rest. She tried not to cry out when they tied her to a tree. Her arms were stretched so tightly she feared ligaments would be damaged from the rough treatment. She was positive by morning she would have bruises all over from the vicious pinches her attacker seemed to enjoy giving her. If she hadn't been gagged she would have tried to bite him, though the idea of her mouth touching his dirty skin made her stomach churn.

She tried to ignore the man's sniggering and obscene talk about her as she stared up at the sky, which was sheathed in clouds.

I refuse to be a prisoner dragged all over these mountains by the two good ol' boys who think ain't is an important part of the English language, she thought, indulging in a session of self-pity. *I would really appreciate it if someone would come rescue me. Right now, I wouldn't care if he looks like a gorilla as long as he bathes regularly and knows what a toothbrush is for. I'd even marry him.* She took a deep breath. *I'm sure if I think about this hellish nightmare long enough, I'll be able to find a way to blame this entire fiasco on Jed. And once I make sure it's all his fault, I'll feel much better about it.*

Chapter 3

Jed's eyes burned with fatigue by the time he arrived at the outskirts of the tiny mountain town. He had finished the last of the coffee twenty miles back. All he could think about was falling onto a bed and sleeping for the next week. But he knew there would be no sleep for him for some time.

As he looked up at the mountains, he saw the tips shrouded in mist and clouds. He thought of Shelby up there somewhere, in the power of two cruel men. Jed refused to even think what they might be doing to her. All he knew was that he wouldn't be happy until he'd killed them so slowly they'd be begging for death. He had already made himself a promise that if she was harmed, the two men would not come back down the mountain alive. Once he finished with them, even the animals would be lucky to find a few scattered remains.

He pulled into the sheriff's station parking lot and stopped the car. He rubbed his hands over his face, grimacing at the bristly feel of his beard. His clothing was wrinkled beyond repair and he felt in dire need of a long hot shower.

The deputy at the front desk couldn't have been twenty-five. He looked up as Jed entered the station. "Can I help you?" he asked warily.

"I'm Jed Hawkins. Here about the Carlisle abduction." Jed pulled out his wallet and showed the man not only his driver's license, but also his government ID. "I'm supposed to see a Deputy Rick Howard here."

The officer's eyes widened as he gazed at the ID. "He hasn't come in yet. But Sheriff Rainey is here. He can talk to you about it."

"Who's in charge of the rescue team out looking for Ms. Carlisle?" Jed rasped, looking around. He found things just a little too quiet for his taste. "What leads have your people turned up? Does anyone have an idea who might have broken into the Ackerman cabin? Or why they took Ms. Carlisle? What about Ms. Ackerman? What's her condition?"

The deputy fairly leapt for the telephone. "I'm sure the sheriff can tell you that." The moment his call connected, he conducted a hurried conversation with the person on the other end. Then he flashed Jed a sickly grin. "The sheriff'll be right out."

Jed stood by the door looking outside. One woman had been brutally attacked, another kidnapped. He didn't want to think that no one was out there looking for Shelby. Damn them!

"Would you like some coffee, Mr. Hawkins?" the deputy ventured.

"What I'd like are some answers!" he snapped, then relented. After all, he couldn't blame this kid for someone else's incompetence. But if Jed didn't receive the answers he wanted to hear, heads would roll.

"Mornin', Allen. And this must be Mr. Hawkins. Mr. Hawkins, I'm Sheriff Rainey."

Jed turned to find a mountain of a man dressed in khaki standing before him. Jed shook his hand only because it was the civilized thing to do. Yet the longer he was up here, the less civilized he felt.

"I'm up here on Warren Carlisle's behalf, to find out what search efforts have been made to find his daughter," he told the older man. "Have your people been able to talk to Ms. Ackerman? Were you able to get any kind of description of the men from her?"

The sheriff headed for his office and gestured for Jed to follow.

"Now you have to understand, Mr. Hawkins, this is a small town and we don't have all the resources of a big city. Sometimes you need to have a little patience," he drawled, settling his bulk into his office chair. "Naturally, we're very worried about Ms. Carlisle, and we have calls in to the right people."

Jed restrained himself from gnashing his teeth. "Patience is a virtue, Sheriff." He resisted sneering as he dropped into the visitor's chair. "I have no virtues. What the hell is going on here?"

The older man shifted uneasily in his chair. "Well now, Mr. Hawkins, that's what I'm trying to tell you."

Jed jumped to his feet and leaned forward, planting his hands on top of the desk. If there was one thing he could do very well, it was "in your face" intimidation. Right now he was doing an excellent job of it.

"No friggin' 'well now,' Sheriff," he snarled. "I want answers. Mr. Carlisle wants answers. So far I haven't heard one damn thing from you but excuses. This does not make me happy. I'm not a pleasant person when I'm not happy."

Sheriff Rainey's shoulders rose and fell in a large sigh. "We don't have much to go on because we couldn't find any signs to follow. It's as if the mountain just swallowed them up."

Jed felt an icy cold penetrate his veins. "What about dogs? A good tracking dog can pick up the faintest of scents."

"Our regular tracker and his dog are out on another job. There's a kid lost somewhere at the other end of the county," he finally admitted. "The tracker probably won't be back for another two days. We plan to send him out then."

Jed spun around in a tight circle. His hands flexed with the need to wreak mayhem. He wanted something to punch, and right now the sheriff was a likely target. As if the older man sensed the dangerous direction of Jed's thoughts, he scooted his chair back a bit. He couldn't miss the murder written on Jed's dark features.

It took a great deal of effort but Jed finally got his temper under control. "By then the scent will be gone. Especially if you get any rain. We're talking about a defenseless woman at the mercy of two, maybe more, men," he said softly, but the menace was still there. "Judging from what little I've heard, these are men who obviously have no conscience. With animals like them around, you can't be bothered to pick up the phone and demand another tracker? You couldn't have informed Mr. Carlisle of your problem? Believe me, he would have had anything you needed at your disposal immediately."

Sheriff Rainey quailed under Jed's wrath. "We thought our tracker would be back before you—you showed up," he stammered. Then, as if finally realizing he was the one who should be in charge, he straightened up and fixed Jed with a steely glare. "Now listen here, Hawkins. What we're talkin' about has nothing to do with those white-collar crimes you see in the city. If these men are who we think they are, they've done this before. At least four women have been reported missing in the area in the past two years..." He realized his error the moment he spoke.

Jed's eyes had turned cold and hard. On his face was the expression of a man who could kill without breaking into a sweat. "What are you trying to tell me, Sheriff? That this has happened before?" His soft tones could have cut through stainless steel.

The officer shifted uneasily in his chair, which suddenly seemed too small for his bulky body. "Well now, we don't have rock-hard evidence these same men are responsible for kidnapping other women," he said hastily. "One of the rangers thinks so and one of my men has a hunch about it. But there's nothing we can do until we come up with some proof."

"Did you post any warnings? Did you suggest that women alone be more careful because of these abductions?'' Jed's smile was deadly. "No, of course you didn't. You wouldn't want to scare off the tourists who visit your lovely little hamlet. After all, your town relies heavily on tourism, and many families have vacation homes up here. You're not going to want to run off your main source of revenue, are you? Tell me something, did you do *anything?* Did you suggest to your town council that you hire more deputies? Run more patrols?'' Each word sliced the air. "What about checking on anyone who lives a ways out of town? Especially if those people are women living alone?'' Jed's voice was laced with disgust. "No, you didn't, did you?''

"Our town's crime rate is very low,'' Sheriff Rainey argued, his florid face turning even redder with agitation.

Jed couldn't miss the man's defensive gestures. He'd guess the sweat rings under the sheriff's arms and the way he fidgeted in his chair proved he was in the wrong, but that he thought what the hell, there was nothing he could do about it. Jed had never felt more violent than he did at that moment. He forced thoughts of Shelby out of his mind. If he took even one second to think about what she might be suffering right now, there would be dire consequences for the man sitting before him.

Sheriff Rainey wasn't about to fool with this man. With black jeans that had seen better days, scuffed boots, a black T-shirt and his dark hair hanging loosely around his shoulders, Jed looked like someone who should be locked up in one of the cells in the back of the building instead of confronting the law. But there was a sense of leashed power in his stance.

"I want to talk to that deputy. I also want to talk to the ranger," Jed said abruptly.

"Rick, you out there?" the sheriff called. Hearing a faint response, he shouted, "Then get in here!" There was no masking his relief that Jed's attention would be directed at another victim.

A khaki-clad man in his late twenties appeared in the doorway. He nodded toward Jed. "You wanted me, Sheriff?"

"This is Jed Hawkins. He wants anything you have on that break-in at the Ackerman place and that woman who was kidnapped," the man rumbled.

The deputy glanced at Jed. "I've been expecting you."

Jed turned back to the sheriff. "Let me make something very clear to you," he said in a low, deadly voice. "If anything has happened to Shelby Carlisle because you couldn't be bothered to admit you needed help, I will turn into your worst enemy. You won't want to see me again, believe me."

The older man glared. "Is that a threat, Hawkins?"

Jed's face didn't change expression. "No, it's a promise." He turned around and left the small office, the deputy at his heels.

As the two men headed for the outer door, the officer looked at Jed. "You look as if you could use some breakfast."

"It might sop up a few gallons of coffee I've drunk," he admitted, then lowered his voice. "Any place where we can talk without the sheriff barging in and further ruining my day?"

The man nodded. "Come on." He grabbed a hand-held radio receiver and ambled out. "It's within walking distance."

He didn't say another word until they were seated in a rear booth at a nearby restaurant with steaming cups of coffee set in front of them.

"I could tell the sheriff isn't exactly on your top-ten list." Rick Howard grinned.

"Top five most wanted." Jed grimaced. "What the hell is going on around here?"

Rick lowered his voice. "Election year is coming up and the old man wants to make sure he's reelected. The best way is to keep these disappearances under wraps. It's helped that the other women apparently didn't have any family looking for them. None of them were locals. Seems these guys know better than to snatch anyone who has family up here."

Jed felt the muscles in his stomach tighten. "How many others have been taken?"

The deputy paused. "Four. That we know of. I have a feeling there's been more, though."

"How do you know about the four?" Jed leaned back as the waitress set his plate in front of him. He looked at the stack of hotcakes with eggs on the side and wondered if he'd manage to eat any of it.

"Pure luck. Although we did find one woman's backpack. It had been thrown in some bushes. We're not sure if she left it there in hopes someone would find it or what. It gave us her name and address. All we found out was that she had headed this way on vacation. She was never found."

"And?" Jed dutifully applied himself to his food. With what he figured was ahead of him he'd need all the strength he could get.

"Bill Weaver, out at the Big Pines ranger station, has come across these guys high up in the mountains a couple times. They always claim they're only up there hiking, but Bill figures they're living up there even though it's illegal. The one who seems to be the leader is Eric Porter, one of those Vietnam vets who refused to believe the war was over. His two nephews are up there with him." He shook his head. "If you want, I'll have you talk to Bill next. What I can tell you is those guys are a bunch of really bad customers who know everything there is to know about weapons and living in the wild. No one wants to go up against them. Plus they've lived up there so long they know the mountains like the back of their hands. So far no one's been able to find out where they hole up. I mean it. These guys are bad news."

Jed determinedly forked up a piece of egg and put it in his mouth. He chewed and swallowed. "You want to talk about bad? Those bastards haven't met me yet."

Jed was relieved that Bill Weaver turned out to be as no nonsense as Rick. In his early forties, he had skin the color of leather and the manner of a man who was happier when he was outdoors.

"You really going to try to track those SOBs?" Bill asked, looking at Jed through narrowed blue eyes.

Jed stared back. "Not just try. I'm going to do it."

Bill still studied him. "You got Indian in ya?"

Jed tried not to smile. "Some Apache from way back."

The older man nodded. "They're good trackers. I tell you, you're going to need whatever you got inside you to find these guys. The uncle is one of those survivalists who's happier living out there in the wild where he can pretend he's still at war with someone. Most people don't remember that he grew up around here. He spent his childhood up in the hills hunting with his dad and brothers until he joined the army. Because of his experience, the army dropped him behind enemy lines for months at a time. Probably because of that he's now more animal than human. His nephews are dumber'n dirt. They didn't believe in doing a day's work so they moved up with him a few years ago."

"Around the time women started disappearing?" Jed guessed.

The ranger nodded. A grim expression tightened his facial muscles. "I'd say within six months."

Jed walked over to an area map covering one of the cabin's walls. He studied it as if committing it to memory.

"You have a good rifle with you?" Bill asked.

Jed was still absorbed in the map. "I have what's needed. Where's the Ackerman cabin on this?"

Bill pointed to a spot on the map. "I tried to do some tracking as soon as it got light this morning, but I lost them almost immediately. From what signs I could read, it looked as if they were headed northeast. Those boys might have been able to hide their tracks, but I can't imagine they can hide the woman's as well unless they keep a close eye on her the whole time. You might get lucky.''

Jed nodded, still gazing at the map. "They're going to learn they grabbed the wrong woman this time.''

The ranger hadn't thought there was anyone alive who could go up against those bastards and live. But what he saw in Jed's storm-colored eyes convinced him he was wrong.

Next Jed stopped by the local hospital, where Meredith was recovering from her attack. What he found was a subdued brunette with a black eye and bruises around her throat.

"I'm sorry, Jed," she said tearfully, as he covered her hands with his warm grasp and asked how she was doing. "I feel as if it was my fault."

He shook his head. "No, don't feel that way. I'm just glad to know you're all right."

"But the sheriff said other women have been kidnapped and never returned!"

He privately damned the man for upsetting her with information she didn't need. "Don't even think about that. I'm going to get her back, Meredith."

She studied him long and hard. Especially his choice of clothing. "I believe you will. Something tells me there's more to you than meets the eye." She managed a weak smile. "I'll tell you one thing I didn't tell the sheriff, since I didn't think it would do any good. One of those bastards has a chipped front tooth. Give him special hell from me."

He grinned. "I will." He dropped a kiss on her forehead. "You just concentrate on getting better. Was your family notified?"

She nodded. "I told them to stay in Rome. I made it sound like nothing more than my getting mugged."

"Then if you need anything, call Mr. Carlisle's office and they'll take care of it for you." He extracted a business card and laid it on her bedside table. "When you're discharged from here, I'll arrange to have someone drive you back to L.A. I don't want you staying up here alone."

"Thanks. I don't think I'd want to stay up here, either." She watched him start to leave the room. "You really love her, don't you?"

He stopped in the doorway. "Let's just say Shelby Carlisle and I have unfinished business to settle." With that, he left.

Meredith started to smile, but quickly discovered the action hurt. "Now why couldn't I have found someone like him?"

Shelby was starving. Her stomach was growling so loudly she was positive the entire mountain could hear it. Along with that, her arms ached from being pulled as the two men practically dragged her up the trail. But worst of all were her feet, which she feared had blisters on top of blisters. She wasn't sure she could take another step and right about then decided she didn't want to. At least they'd taken that disgusting rag out of her mouth. She was positive she'd never forget the taste of the filthy cloth. She had no hope of screaming for help up here. After all, who would hear her other than any wild animal roaming around, and she already had two wild animals in her company, thank you very much.

"Do you mind?" She tried to dig in her heels, but that only made her feet hurt more. She pulled on the rope wrapped around her wrists, then almost fell as the man holding the end, who was built like a tree, kept going. "Excuse me, I'd like to take a rest! Hey!" she yelped, sliding a few more feet before her captor finally stopped.

"What's your problem now?" he impatiently demanded. "We've got a long ways to go without listening to your bitching every step of the way."

"Then maybe you should set me free before I really get on your nerves." Shelby refused to be the least bit intimidated by his dark scowl. In fact, she shot a glare back at him. She wasn't pleased to learn he wasn't intimidated by hers, either. "Okay, I'm not exactly dealing with Harvard graduates here. Since I left the alphabet blocks at home, let me put it to you as simply as I can. I haven't eaten since yesterday, I'm positive my arms have stretched a foot since last night, my feet are killing me, and most of all, I have to go to the bathroom!" she finally shouted. Angry tears threatened to fall, but she refused to allow them. She had already figured out that tears would not appeal to these men's better instincts. Assuming they had any.

He started toward her, his hand out as if he was going to strike her.

"Don't do it, Chris!" his brother warned. "We want her to look real pretty for Eric. He wouldn't like it if you hurt her."

Chris glared at his brother. "Yeah, well, he ain't gonna like the mouth she's got on her."

Andy grinned. "He'll take care of that."

Shelby felt the bottom of her stomach fall even farther as the men leered at her. She wished her shorty pajamas covered more of her.

"Look, I'm not going anywhere," she said wearily. "I don't even know where I am. But I would like a couple minutes' privacy."

Andy looked at Chris. "She could go in those trees over there."

Chris wasn't as friendly about it. "Make sure we can still see the top of your head."

Shelby hated to think what it would take to ensure that. And what would happen if they couldn't see the top of her head.

"Dad, please send someone who is meaner but much smarter than these cretins, so I can go home," she muttered, limping over to the bushes and her scant privacy.

It wasn't long before Chris was again roughly pulling her up the trail, if potholes and rocks half-buried in the earth could be called a trail.

Shelby stumbled along, forcing herself to focus on anything except the horrors that could be in store for her. It wasn't long before Jed's face entered her mind's eye. Just yesterday she would have thrust him out of her thoughts. Today she willingly immersed herself in the memory of the first time he'd kissed her. . . .

They had gone out to dinner and seen a play afterward. The play was new and well received by critics and audience alike. As they sat in the darkened theater and watched the handsome vampire seduce his victim, Shelby felt a warmth steal through her body. She imagined that same warmth moving like an in-

*visible mist to surround Jed. She sat in the seat
watching the vampire give his new lover the forbid-
den kiss and couldn't help wondering what it would
be like if Jed kissed her. When he escorted her back
to her apartment, she soon discovered she wouldn't
have to wait to find out.*

*Only a small lamp was lit in her living room, send-
ing out a faint golden light when they entered. Jed
didn't give her time to turn on any more lights, but
immediately trapped her against the wall, the heat of
his body against hers. He placed a hand on either side
of her, effectively keeping her within his embrace.*

*"When I chose the play I had no idea it would have
such a powerful effect on you," he murmured.*

*She looked up at him, seeing the same bewitching
shadows in his face and eyes. With artless grace, she
raised her head, baring her throat as if offering herself to him.*

*"It would make a woman think twice about invit-
ing a man into her house," she said huskily. "That is
the only way he can enter, isn't it? He has to be invited in?"*

*He dipped his head and touched her earlobe with
the tip of his tongue. It was as if a flame had stroked
her skin as his tongue outlined her ear, then trailed
down to the gentle curve of her jaw. "You invited me
in."*

*"Yes, I did," she whispered, just as his mouth en-
gulfed hers with a heat that seemed to overtake her
body. His tongue plunged between her parted lips
with a silent demand for her to participate. His mouth
made love to her with the same sizzling sensuality she
knew his body would. By the time he lifted his head,*

she was certain her will was no longer her own. From that first kiss, Shelby was Jed's....

She swallowed the sob that threatened to erupt in a torrent of tears as the memories overwhelmed her. Jed was one of the calmest, most controlled men she'd ever known. She couldn't remember ever seeing him lose his temper or act out of sorts. That had bothered her at times, since she felt she had to keep her own fiery nature under wraps—as if she had to prove she could be in as much control of her emotions as he was. And it wasn't always easy! Right now, she wouldn't have minded his icy calm which sometimes made him appear inhuman. Because if she was with Jed, she wouldn't be stuck with these smelly, ugly, rude men who were taking her home as a gift to their uncle.

Jed wasn't surprised to find the Ackerman cabin barely secured. He damned the sheriff again for his sloppy methods and quickly went through the building.

It didn't take him long to get an idea what had been taken other than Shelby. The kitchen was a mess; cabinets and pantry doors had been left open, and there were gaps on shelves where cans and foodstuffs had been taken. The gun cabinet had also been broken into and now stood empty. He went upstairs and easily figured out which bedroom Shelby had used. All he had to do was take one breath and inhale the faint scent of her perfume.

"You didn't go with them easily, did you, love?" he murmured, fingering a chair that lay on its side. He walked back downstairs and out the door in the direction Bill Weaver told him he figured the men had headed. He walked into the wooded area and squatted on his haunches, looking for signs.

"Shelby, my love, when I catch up with you, I'm going to make sure you don't get caught up with something like this ever again," he said grimly.

Jed began following the trail. Luckily, Shelby was holding the two men back. He doubted she would be able to keep up with them for long. Thanks to her, he hoped to catch up to them by the end of the day. The first thing he planned to do was beat the hell out of those two men for taking his woman.

Jed carried little with him—not because he couldn't handle the extra weight, but in deference to how quickly he intended to travel up the rocky trail. He settled for a canteen, a knapsack filled with lightweight food and a rifle. A deadly hunting knife was sheathed inside his boot.

As he climbed, his stride as graceful as a mountain lion's, he kept his mind centered on one thing: Shelby. He recalled the scent of her skin when heated by their passion. The feel of her body under his fingertips as he tracked every inch of her slender form. He recalled watching her stroke scented body lotion on her legs and arms in that slow, leisurely way she knew drove him out of his mind. Then he remembered how her facial expression changed when he took the bottle from her hands and began smoothing lotion over her body in even more languorous strokes. It was never long before she pulled him down beside her.

He gritted his teeth as he felt his desire rise with the erotic thoughts roaring through his head. His stride lengthened as he forced himself to keep going.

But thoughts of Shelby refused to leave his head. Especially that first time they made love....

The evening had been filled with laughter. From the moment Jed arrived to pick Shelby up for their date, he planned to make love to her that night. Little did he know that fate was working very hard against him. It began with their dinner reservation somehow disappearing off the books; even Jed's persuasive manner couldn't budge the maitre d' into finding a table for them. The club they were going to after dinner was closed due to an electrical fire, and Jed's car was towed away. Naturally, when he called for a cab he was told it could be an hour's wait. Perhaps it was pure luck that a cab happened to be cruising the area; he wasted no time in flagging it down. After that, Jed wondered if he wouldn't be better off dropping her at her apartment and going home to sulk. Or perhaps even damage a few walls with his fist.

"Come in for a drink," Shelby invited as she unlocked her front door. She smiled and stepped back. After he'd discovered there had been two robberies in her building in the last few months, he'd insisted on going through her apartment before allowing her inside.

"Are you sure it's safe?" he asked sardonically. "For all we know, that big earthquake might hit at any moment."

She laughed. "Oh, let's continue to tempt fate, shall we? Besides, I've been thinking of doing some redecorating anyway."

Shelby wore a bronze silk slip dress that skimmed her body. Spaghetti straps bared her arms and shoulders, while the short length revealed even more of her.

*Strappy high-heeled sandals in a matching color
showed off her spectacular legs. She had pulled her
hair up into a loose pouf anchored with a bronze-
colored clip. Jed ached to steal the clip in order to
watch her hair tumble down around her shoulders.
He wondered what she used to cause her skin to
sparkle under the light.*

He sat down on the couch.

*"Are you sure this thing won't collapse?" he asked,
still uneasy that something else might happen.*

*Her laughter stole over him like sparkling water.
"It has been an interesting evening, hasn't it?" She
brought over a glass of whiskey, neat, and handed it
to him. With her wineglass in the other hand, she sat
down next to him.*

*Jed kept his eyes on his glass instead of on the en-
ticing length of thigh so close to him. "Not exactly
what I planned," he grumbled.*

*Her eyes sparkled with the same laughter. "And
what did you plan, Jed?"*

*He lifted his free hand and stroked her cheek. "The
kind of night neither one of us would ever forget."*

Jed swallowed his groan as the memories continued to pour forth. He was surprised he didn't walk
into a tree as he proceeded blindly up the trail. He
muttered a curse, but it didn't stop the images from
continuing to tempt his senses. How had she managed to insinuate herself so deeply into his soul?

*She felt like silk, the coolness of her skin rapidly
heating up the longer he touched her. And once he
started, he could never stop touching her. Couldn't*

stop savoring the feel of her skin under his mouth and hands.

He could hear the soft snick of the zipper on her dress as he lowered the tab until it stopped just below her waist. He swore under his breath when he discovered she wasn't wearing a bra and that the pair of scanty bikini panties she had on covered little. The fluttery touch of her hands against his chest as she unbuttoned his shirt was enough to make him explode. But that wasn't what he wanted. He wanted to bury himself deep inside her and never leave her.

"Not here," he said hoarsely, pulling himself back before he fully succumbed.

Shelby stood up, allowing her dress to drop to the carpet. She smiled and snagged the ends of his tie, which was still around his neck.

"Come with me," she ordered in a voice that sounded more like a purr. She tugged on the tie and led him toward her bedroom.

There was no more talking after that. Only whispers in the dark as she told him what she liked and his groans each time she touched him. She was all silken heat with erotic hip movements that set his blood afire.

By morning, Jed felt as if he had been wrung out to dry.

Until a sleepy-eyed Shelby touched him again.

Jed cursed. He had to stop doing this! He peered upward, searching for any hint of flame-colored hair. In these woods he had hoped the vivid color would beckon to him like a banner. But he suspected it wouldn't be that easy.

"That fiery soul better keep you going, Shelby," he muttered, as he moved around a large boulder blocking his path. "Don't let them drag you down, Shel. Be strong for me. I'm coming for you, love."

Chapter 4

"That's it! If I walk any more I won't have feet left!" Shelby shrieked, pulling hard on the rope. It hadn't been long since they'd stopped for a quick break. The men had eagerly consumed some of the food stolen from Meredith's cabin, but Shelby wasn't offered one bite. When they were ready to go again, Chris looped the rope around Shelby's wrists and pulled her along, still using the rope as a leash. Now she gritted her teeth against the pain as she dug in her heels.

"Listen to me, bitch, you'll go where we tell you to go and when we tell you to go and I don't care how tired your feet are." A scowling Chris advanced on her. "I'm sick and tired of your fancy-lady bitchin'. You're going to learn to do what we tell you when we tell you or you're going to be in a heap of trouble by the time we get up to the cabin. You keep this up and you'll find yourself crawlin' up that trail on your hands and knees.''

Shelby didn't hear him. By now she was beyond coherent thought. She hadn't eaten in more than twenty-four hours, her feet burned with pain and her wrists were raw from the rope rubbing against her delicate skin. She decided the only reason they had taken off her gag was because they didn't think anyone would hear if she screamed. That thought frightened her more than anything. She decided that if that was to be her fate, she was bound and determined to inflict her share of pain before she went down for good. She twisted to her side and kicked out with the intention of doing damage to Chris. What she didn't expect was that he anticipated her attack and swiftly grabbed her foot, instantly throwing her off-balance. If he hadn't held on to her foot, she would surely have fallen on her back. His leering grin promised punishment for her rash action.

"Thought you'd get me where it counted, didn't ya, bitch?'' he said hoarsely, roughly twisting her ankle to one side until her face contorted with pain. This time she did fall down. "Looks as if I'll have to teach you some manners before we meet up with Uncle Eric. I wouldn't want him to think we gave him a woman who didn't know her place.''

Shelby's eyes widened as agony shot up her leg. With his body strength and large hands, she knew it wouldn't take much for the man to break a few bones.

"Chris, you can't!'' Andy warned, pushing Shelby's leg out of Chris's grip.

"She was gonna kick me in the crotch!'' he shouted.

Andy ran over to Shelby and took hold of her bound wrists, pulling her to her feet. "You can't make Chris mad," he advised her in a low voice. "He don't have lots of patience."

"Yes, I gathered that," she muttered between clenched teeth, wincing as the pain from her jarred spine continued to penetrate her equally sore muscles. "I'm just hungry and thirsty and tired, and I wish you'd let me go. Believe me, I wouldn't tell anyone about either of you. Even if I did, I doubt anyone would believe I was taken by two escapees from a B movie."

Andy looked confused. "Huh?"

Shelby rolled her eyes. "Forget it, okay?" She shrugged her shoulders to ease the strain on them. "I should have realized you wouldn't have cable TV this high up."

"We're goin'!" Chris shouted.

Andy looked over his shoulder. "Maybe we should let her have a drink of water."

"All she needs is a good beatin' to show her who's boss. We're goin' now!"

"Terrific. Not only refugees from a bad movie, but from the Cro-Magnon period as well," she muttered.

She felt uneasy when Chris advanced on her. "You think I don't know you're insultin' us with some of those big words you're usin'?" he told her in a low voice that fairly rumbled with fury. His sour breath made her wrinkle her nose in distaste. "You think we're all dumb hicks, doncha? Let me tell ya, we're not. We may not know all the words you use or have fancy houses, but we know things up here that could get a body killed if they're not careful."

Shelby wanted nothing more than to plop down on the ground and cower under his fury. She felt so afraid inside that she was positive her insides had turned to jelly, but she couldn't allow him to see how frightened she was and fought back the only way she knew how—with words. "You know, a good dose of dental hygiene would do wonders for you," she said glibly. "Unless, of course, you prefer to kill people with your breath."

This time he didn't strike her across the face, but used one leg to sweep hers out from under her. She landed on her bruised spine again.

"Chris!" Andy cried.

Chris pushed his face close to Shelby's. "You better learn some manners real fast, little girl," he warned her. "Cuz Uncle Eric don't have the patience I do and he's a lot meaner than I am." He suddenly began staring over her head.

Shelby looked uneasy. "What?" She suddenly wished she hadn't asked that question.

"That hair's too bright and could be seen a long ways off. If a 'copter flies overhead, they'll find her just cuz of that hair." He pulled his billed cap off his head and slapped it on hers. "This should hide it."

Shelby cringed at the thought of Chris's dirty cap covering her head. "I hope you don't have lice," she muttered.

She stood her ground when he lifted his hand. She was positive that if he hit her, he'd probably break a bone. She was prepared not to cry out. She wouldn't allow him the satisfaction. And when she got a chance she was going to make sure *he* suffered great pain for what he was doing to her. She wasn't sure what she was going to do yet, but she knew it would be horrible.

Only Andy tugging on his brother's arm saved Shelby's face from damage. She exhaled a silent sigh of relief when the younger man was able to pull Chris away.

"We gotta move," Andy told him. "Uncle Eric's waitin' for us." He shot a quick glance at Shelby. "We ain't got all that far to go now. And we don't want to make him mad."

Chris shot Shelby a glare that promised punishment big-time if she dared open her mouth again. At that moment, she fervently vowed not to say another word.

There has to be someone coming after me, she thought as she trudged upward, every step causing more pain. *Dad would have hired someone to find me. I know he would.*

The thought of her father was the only thing keeping her going. Shelby silently prayed Warren wasn't worrying too much about her. She prayed he was remembering to take his blood-pressure medication. The last thing he needed was to get sick because he was worrying about her.

Then Jed came to mind. She knew he had to be back by now. He wouldn't leave the older man's side.

He would assure him Shelby would be all right.

Jed found the signs fairly easy to read. He could see that the higher they climbed, the less the men bothered to hide their tracks. Were they that positive they weren't being followed? Or did they think no one would bother going any farther? After meeting the town's sorry excuse for a sheriff, Jed could well understand their arrogance. He squatted down, examining the faint drag marks in the dry earth. He was grateful there hadn't been any rain recently to ruin the trail for him. Judging from the signs, he hazarded a guess that Shelby was tied and one of the men was pulling on a rope, sometimes dragging her. After a while he noticed the marks had changed, as if her stride had altered. Her steps must be causing her pain now. He exhaled a sharp breath.

"Bastards don't have any idea what's coming after them," he muttered. "Hang on, Shelby." By sheer force of will, he kept a mental picture of her in his mind. He was feeling the effects of long hours in the air, little sleep, even less food. He doubted he'd have a chance to sleep until he had Shelby in his arms again. He prayed that, with luck, it wouldn't take long.

Ordinarily, Jed would have relished a climb like this. He always enjoyed the outdoors and physical exercise, and this would have been a wonderful challenge for a weekend, when he could relax enough to enjoy the crisp air, the rock-littered trail and the vibrant nature all around him. Now his challenge was finding the men climbing ahead of him.

Since there weren't any signs of a third man, Jed guessed they'd be meeting up with him soon. Jed only hoped he could snatch Shelby back before then. The odds didn't bother him, but he knew the moment he snatched Shelby back those two men would be hot on their heels, so he and Shelby would have to move as fast as possible.

Naturally, that would depend on what condition he found Shelby in. If he didn't like what he saw, they'd be lucky if they weren't left scattered in pieces across the mountain.

Jed prided himself on his unlimited patience. He believed in keeping his emotions in check. He hadn't always done so. His dad hadn't bothered to stick around to see him born, and his mother hadn't wanted him. He'd grown up in a series of foster homes because his grandparents decided they couldn't deal with an angry kid who vented his rage on whatever dared cross his path.

If it hadn't been for the time he was caught boosting a car, ironically owned by a DEA agent, Jed probably would have secured his higher education from the state's prison system. But the agent saw what was really inside the angry teen and kicked his butt when it was needed. If it hadn't been for him, Jed might have been dead before he turned twenty-one.

Instead of ending up on the wrong side of the law, he wore fine clothes, was invited into socially correct households and traveled to the world's hot spots whenever his special skills were needed.

The man who always appeared so calm to the outside world was highly proficient in the silent kill, whether it be via knife or his hands. He knew enough about explosives to blow up whatever needed destroying and he could slip in and out of countries like a ghost.

Now, Jed found his temper rising rapidly, a raw and bitter feeling. He had found it difficult to con-

tain his anger as he dealt with the local law agency
and had chafed at the delays. He was sure Sheriff
Rainey and his colleagues questioned why Warren
Carlisle had sent Jed out here. After all, he wasn't
familiar with the country and didn't give the appearance of a man who lived in the wild. Yet Warren had
known that if anyone could find his daughter, it
would be Jed Hawkins.

Jed stopped at a bush that had had several branches
broken off it fairly recently. He was catching up to
them.

He looked up when he heard an eagle's shriek
overhead. He swore under his breath when he heard
a rifle shot ring out.

"Damn you," he muttered. His features darkened
with a fury he didn't bother to tamp down even when
he saw that the marksman had missed and the eagle
had flown off to safety. Jed would nurture his anger
and use it when the time was right.

"What are you doing?" Shelby shrieked at Chris,
who had his rifle braced against his shoulder. Since
his first shot at the eagle had missed, he was going to
try again. She pushed against him, forcing him off-
balance.

He spun around, about to strike at her with the
stock of his rifle when Andy grasped his arm.

"What the hell you doin'?" the younger man
shouted.

"I'm sick and tired of her mouth!" Chris shouted
back. "And don't start in yammerin' about Uncle
Eric again, you hear? I only plan to take some skin

off her. Then she won't be so high and mighty. And she'll still be good for somethin'."

"Fine, boy, why don't you tell me why Andy's so upset about what I might learn?"

At the sound of a man's raspy voice, the three-some turned around and looked upward.

The moment Shelby saw the man standing on the boulder above them, her hopes of either escape or rescue sank like a stone.

Legs widespread, shoulders back, he was dressed in camouflage fatigues and hiking boots, with a heavy-duty rifle slung over his shoulder. It wasn't just his appearance that destroyed her peace of mind, it was the feral expression on his narrow face as he looked down on her. His body was whipcord lean, with skin the dark bronze of someone who lived outdoors. A nasty-looking scar angled down his right cheek. She wasn't sure, but she judged him to be in his midfor-ties. Sandy brown hair was cut so short she imagined she could see his scalp. His sleeves were rolled up to his biceps, revealing corded muscle and a coiled ser-pent tattooed with the name and number of a marine division under its deadly looking fangs. She thought "Uncle Eric" might be a little cleaner than his neph-ews, but not all that much.

She had no doubt she was looking at a man who had no scruples, didn't own anything close to a con-science. She forced herself not to shiver in fright or give any kind of reaction to his stare because she sensed that was what he wanted from her—he wanted to feed off her fear. His washed-out, hazel eyes held no expression whatsoever. The man she looked at was the embodiment of her worst fear: a man with no soul.

He was the kind of creature who would think nothing of eating his young.

Out of the corner of her eye she could see Chris's expression waver between pure fear and an eagerness to please as he faced his uncle.

"Look what we found for ya, Uncle Eric." He gave Shelby such a hard push between her shoulder blades that she stumbled and fell forward.

She mentally added a couple of skinned knees to her list of aches and pains. A tiny voice inside her head warned her not to say anything that would get her in any more trouble. But she wasn't about to start listening to that voice.

"Honestly, Uncle Eric, can't you teach your boys any manners?" she drawled, sitting back on her heels, then rising to her feet in one graceful motion. "It's bad enough they dragged me out of a comfortable bed in the middle of the night. Then they couldn't even be bothered to find me shoes that fit." She lifted one leg. Faint streaks of blood showed on top of her foot, which was jammed in a loafer that was obviously too small. "I must say this trip hasn't been one of my most memorable."

Eric's face darkened with fury as he turned on his nephews. "What the hell is she talking about?"

Chris looked uneasy. "We knew Ellen wasn't doin' too well and that you'd need someone new to replace her real soon," he explained. "This pretty lady and a friend were in the cabin we broke into. We would have brought them both, but the friend fought back, so I hit her and she fell against a piece of furniture. Don't worry, I made sure she wouldn't tell anybody about us," he hastily assured the older man.

Shelby's heart dropped all the way to her ankles. His statement had to mean Meredith was dead. Still, after what Shelby had been hearing, her friend might be better off than she was. She dreaded to think what good ol' Uncle Eric might need her for. Something told her it wouldn't be purely for her cooking and cleaning skills. The idea of his touching her sent disgust roiling through her veins.

Eric climbed down the rocks with the agility of a mountain goat. He jumped the final distance and landed squarely on his feet. He walked over to Chris and, before any of them could blink, backhanded the younger man. Chris staggered from the blow. He wiped his nose with his hand, which came away bloody.

"You took somebody who lived down there?" Eric's quiet voice whipped across the younger man like a laser. "You know we never bother with anyone who lives down there. We don't want any more trouble than we already have."

"No one's gonna tell the cops," the younger man argued back. "No one ever has before."

"That's because we always picked up women who didn't matter. Hitchhikers with no family are one thing—the cops never care about what happens to them as long as no one asks about them. A woman like her is something else," Eric stated coldly. "Look at her, you idiots. That's not discount-store clothing she's wearing." He walked over to Shelby and roughly pulled off Chris's cap. "Someone's going to be coming up here hunting for her! And if I had a woman who looked like this I'd do whatever I had to to get her back. You idiot!''

"My father will want me back!" Shelby hastily interjected, then wished she hadn't when Eric turned his attention to her. "He has money. He'll pay for my safe return. I know he will."

Eric reached out and touched her hair with his fingertips. "Color this rich has to be real," he murmured, rubbing it between his fingers. He glanced down, studying the lightly tanned skin bared by the low-cut pajama top. His gaze dropped farther to her legs. His fingertips slid down her throat and lingered on her shoulder. "Soft. Real soft. Like silk." He picked up one of her hands and turned it over, so he could study her palm. "Not the skin of a woman who has to work for a living."

Shelby found it difficult to swallow the lump lodged in her throat. She was feeling too uncomfortable with the heat that was quickly rising in his gaze. She suddenly knew what it felt like to be a fawn caught by a cougar.

"My father would pay to have me returned unharmed," she said, stressing the last word.

"Now how do you know you might not rather stay around here with us? We're likable people." Eric Porter lifted a strand of her hair and admired the color.

With him standing so close to her she realized he didn't smell any better than his nephews. She tried not to gag at his body odor and forced herself not to step back from him.

Doesn't anyone understand the use of soap and water around here?

"Look, I told your little boys already." She forced herself to keep her voice low and even. She sensed showing fear or revulsion would only amuse these men. "I'm not meant for outdoor life. My idea of roughing it is a hotel that doesn't have room service."

Eric moved closer. "You'll get used to it. We'll stay here tonight." He looked up at the sky. "It'd be dark by the time we got to the cabin and I wouldn't want this pretty lady to take a wrong step and fall off the cliff while we're climbing up there." His grin held a malice that was pure evil. "I'd sure hate to lose her so soon."

Shelby swallowed the nausea rising in her throat at the look in his eyes.

In the movies, my hero would be striding in right this moment to rescue me, she thought wildly. *Three-against-one odds aren't all that bad.*

"Sh..." Jed took a deep breath as he stared at the group standing in the clearing. "I didn't think he'd show up so soon," he muttered under his breath. He could deal with the odds, but he would have preferred two against one.

He looked around and realized the shadows were growing longer; the sun was going down. He could only hope that they'd decide to camp there for the night. He had an idea their living quarters weren't all that close by and that the third man had just happened upon them by accident. If they did camp there, it would give Jed a chance to spirit Shelby away sometime during the night. He had found a couple of hiding places along the way and prayed the three men weren't familiar with them. But of course, they knew the area better than he did.

He kept his attention on Shelby. He had to admire her show of bravery with the three men surrounding her like wolves toying with their prey. He also wanted to throttle her for getting in this situation in the first place. This wouldn't have happened if only she had waited for him to come back!

Hidden by the trees and bushes, he feasted his eyes on Shelby. He felt his temper heat up when he noticed the bruise marring one cheek and the cuts and scrapes on her legs and arms. Perhaps the abrasions were due to the mountain climb, but the bruise was obviously caused by a human hand. Right now, Jed wanted to cut off the hand that had struck her. He easily guessed which man deserved punishment. The one called Chris constantly looked at Shelby as if she was a rich dessert he wanted to inhale. Jed vowed Chris wouldn't come through this unscathed if he had anything to do with it.

His biggest surprise was seeing she'd cut her hair.

Why had she done that? He remembered how the flame-colored strands wrapped around him like silken, living fingers when they made love. Now her hair barely touched her neck.

For the moment, Jed was powerless, and he hated that feeling. He knew the only way he could get Shelby out of there safely was to have surprise on his side. For that he would have to wait until full dark. Making no noise, he settled back in his hiding place and watched the three men prepare their camp. One of them tied Shelby to a tree. With any luck, they'd leave her there all night. That would make Jed's job easier. Stealing into a camp with three men had to be a hell of a lot simpler than stealing into a foreign prison to sneak out one of the prisoners. This time, Jed only had to sneak out a feisty redhead and get her home where she belonged. And once they were back in civilization he was going to make damn sure she didn't venture outside the city limits without him!

Shelby rubbed her tongue across her teeth. There was nothing she hated more than to be without toothpaste and soap. She could already tell they weren't something the three men bothered with. It was bad enough that Eric had made dinner. He'd told her he didn't want her to feel too weak from hunger, so he had offered her a healthy portion of the meat. She didn't dare ask what kind it was. The idea of eating Thumper or Bambi was too much for her. She decided this was one time when ignorance was most definitely bliss.

She wasn't even going to consider that Eric was acting kinder than Chris. While the two brothers ate, their uncle untied her hands long enough for her to eat. He offered her choice bits of meat and gave her a tin cup to drink water from. She doubted the cup had ever been washed and forced herself not to think about that, either. At first she feared Eric's kindness meant he expected repayment at bedtime. Luckily, he retied her after the meal and seemed content to keep her tied to the tree for the night, even if he did enjoy talking about what would happen once they got up to the family cabin. She vowed they'd have to kill her first.

For once she wasn't going to complain about the bark snagging in her hair when, as soon as the meal was over, her arms were once more wrapped around the trunk behind her. She hated the way Eric and Chris looked at her outthrust breasts as she sat back against the tree. She was grateful Andy seemed bashful and rarely looked at her, but she also knew she couldn't count on him for help if things got bad.

"Once we get up to the cabin, you can have yourself a nice hot bath and you can stay in the water as long as you want," Eric promised her as he adjusted the rope. He took his time getting the knots just right and "accidentally" touching the sides of her breasts as he looped the rope around her chest to secure her against the tree.

Shelby didn't miss the unholy gleam in his eye or his less-than-subtle groping of her breast. She gritted her teeth, fervently wishing she could land a good kick where it counted. But her memory of Chris's retaliation was too fresh in her mind. While Chris had only threatened to break her foot, she sensed Eric wouldn't hesitate in crushing the bones so she would never walk normally again. Much less be able to run away.

"You actually have running water all the way up here?" she asked, hoping that if she could keep him talking he'd quit touching her. She tried not to squirm when his fingertips brushed across her thigh.

"No, but we have a big tub we can fill with hot water we've heated up over the fire. Course, since you're such a little thing you'll probably want some help getting in and out of the tub," he told her as his eyes hotly raked over her pajama top. The rips in the fabric from her forced trek up the mountain hadn't helped any; he stared at the pale gold skin peeking out from the cottony fabric. "You'll like it up there. It's real private. Only one way in and one way out, and it's not all that easy to find unless you know it's there. Makes it easier to keep away unwanted company." His eyes gleamed.

Shelby's hopes of rescue were rapidly dwindling. She knew what Eric was really telling her. The men lived where they could guarantee no one would be able to sneak up on them.

"What about this Ellen they talked about?" she managed to say in as normal a voice as she could muster. "She might not like having another woman around."

Eric's grin was deadly. "You don't have to worry about Ellen. Where she is she won't mind who's up there."

Shelby felt panic race through her veins in an icy wave. She had no idea who Ellen was, but she suspected the woman was dead. As she herself might well be once Eric got tired of playing his cat-and-mouse games with her. She forced herself not to think about what had happened to Meredith, but the memory kept returning. Shelby vowed she'd find some way to exact revenge for what Chris had done to her friend. Visions of the worst forms of torture began to play through her mind. Before she could stop herself, she began to smile at the idea of Chris hanging by his toes and ants crawling all over his honey-coated body. Unfortunately, Eric happened to catch her smile and viewed it as as a sign of flirtation.

"Hey, don't you worry," he whispered, laying his hand on her shoulder and sliding his fingertips down to the top of her breast. "Those boys aren't going to touch you if I tell them to leave you alone. So you be real nice to me and I'll be real nice to you."

He squeezed her breast so painfully she was certain she'd have bruises there tomorrow.

Shelby refused to show any reaction. When he finally left her, she sagged against the tree. Her fear of the man was so strong she knew she didn't dare go to sleep. Yet if she kept her eyes open, Eric just might come back, and that was the last thing she wanted.

Chapter 5

Jed hadn't missed the exchange as Eric tied Shelby to the tree. He was relieved Eric wasn't keeping her close to him that night and forced his fury down as he listened to Eric hint what his plans for Shelby were.

Now there was no doubt who had kidnapped the other women. The men had obviously been bringing them up here for their own use. And when they grew tired of their toys they discarded them—permanently. For now, Shelby was their newest plaything. The only difference was she had family looking for her.

Jed didn't take his eyes off the group as darkness descended. He noticed the way Eric's gaze kept sliding toward Shelby. Jed silently congratulated her for pretending to be asleep. She was safer that way.

As he waited for the men to doze off, he catalogued their positions around the small campfire in relation to Shelby and mapped out the escape in his head.

He lifted his head, sniffing the air. There was the faint tang of smoke from the fire Andy had just banked, the sharper scent of the pine trees, earthier smells coming from animals who stayed away as long as they could smell man. And there was something else: a hint of moisture in the air. He looked up and saw clouds gathering. It looked as if they would have rain before the night was over.

Jed would have liked nothing more than to feast his eyes on Shelby, but he had to keep his attention on the three men. He felt relief when all three finally fell asleep. They obviously felt secure enough this high up that they didn't need one of them to stand guard. Jed had to give Shelby a lot of credit for having made it this far. It seemed his lady fair was tougher than he'd suspected.

Then he thought back to the last time they were together, when she had more than proven herself to be one tough lady.

If Jed didn't know any better he would have thought he was in love with her.

Shelby was so tired. Her legs ached, her back ached and her feet felt as if they were on fire. The rope looped around her wrists was tied tighter than before and she felt as if all feeling had gone out of her arms. She had been tempted to tell Eric there was no way she could do any more climbing up to the family cabin, thanks to his nephews pushing ill-fitting shoes on her, but she didn't want to give him another chance to touch her. So she gritted her teeth every time she moved her legs or tried to move her arms. She didn't even want to think what contact with the bark was doing to her back and hair, fearing the itching sensation she could feel along her spine had more to do with tiny insects than with wood splinters. To make matters worse, the moment the sun went down, the air grew chilly. She clenched her teeth so they wouldn't chatter with the cold. She was afraid to look down at herself, positive she had turned into one very large goose bump. She drew her sore legs up to her chest in an ineffectual attempt to keep her body heat from escaping.

She was grateful the three men had fallen asleep. She sat back against the tree, watching them roll over and snore. She felt the kind of disgust she would feel if she found three cockroaches in front of her. She only wished she could stomp on them with her too-small shoes until they were nothing more than smudges in the dirt.

"Pigs," she whispered under her breath.

There was nothing, not even a whisper of air, to warn her until a hand settled snugly over her mouth to prevent any outcry.

"Was breaking up with me so rough that you found yourself needing consoling from three men, sweetheart?" The familiar voice was so soft that for a moment she thought she'd imagined it. "No offense, but I thought you would have had better taste than choosing the outdoors type."

She stiffened in her bonds, then tried to turn around, only to find her head kept firmly in place by the restraining hand.

"Don't do anything to wake up the boyfriends," Jed whispered. "Just nod your head if you'd like to get the hell out of here."

She had no problem doing that. She was still stunned to hear his voice. How had Jed made it up here? She couldn't be dreaming, could she?

"Good. Now, I'm going to cut you loose and you're going to have to be as quiet as you possibly can when you creep around the tree. It looks as if those three are pretty heavy sleepers, but I don't intend to give them an excuse to wake up too soon."

Shelby felt the rope lashed around her chest loosen and then fall into her lap. She bit back a moan as white-hot needles of sensation traveled through her arms and legs. She kept herself in a crouched position and, as quietly as possible, crept around the tree. Without thinking, she opened her mouth to ask Jed what he was doing there, but he grasped the back of her head in a firm grip and his mouth covered hers in an all-too-brief but searing kiss.

"No time for more just yet," he murmured in her ear as he took her arm. "We need to get as far away as possible before one of them wakes up and discovers you're gone. Come on." He kept hold of one arm and almost dragged her along behind him.

Even in her stunned state, Shelby couldn't help noticing that Jed didn't look at all the way she was used to seeing him. Gone was the impeccable suit or tuxedo she usually saw him in. Even the renegade ponytail was loosened, with strands of hair falling around his face. His dark clothing seemed to blend in with the forest and she couldn't believe a man could move so swiftly and silently. She imagined she sounded like a herd of elephants as she blindly followed him.

It took only a few steps for the pain to start up in her feet, but she sensed they needed to be a lot farther away before she dared speak. Plus Jed's hold on her wrist was so tight she couldn't have broken from him if she tried. She couldn't imagine where his strength came from.

Oh, she had noticed his lean muscles when she saw him without clothing and knew he ran a minimum of five miles a day, but she couldn't imagine that would prepare him for a duty like this one.

"Please," she gasped finally as she felt a painful stitch in her side.

"We can't stop now," Jed told her in a low voice. "We're still too close to them. I found a cave down a ways, and judging from its condition, I don't think those three ever found it. We can hide in there."

Shelby started to ask him what he was doing here, but his pull on her hand kept her moving at such a quick pace she figured she was better off funneling all her energy into their escape. Every once in a while she looked over her shoulder, as if fearing Eric and his nephews were hot on their heels.

"Why are you here?" she finally managed to ask.

"Not now," he repeated in a grim voice as he quickened his pace.

Shelby kept quiet, concentrating on not stumbling as she hurried to keep up. At last, the stitch in her side refused to be ignored. She pulled back as hard as she could. And was almost yanked off her feet.

Jed spun around, and only his hold on her wrist kept her upright. "What now?" he growled.

"I...can't...go any...farther," she wheezed. "Those idiots had me climbing up here at a killing pace and going down isn't proving to be any easier." She held her aching side with her free hand. "I need a chance to catch my breath."

Jed moved forward until his face was inches from hers. "Listen to me very carefully, because I don't want to say this again. Those men are killers," he said slowly and distinctly. "We can't afford to hang around in case one of them happens to wake up and find you gone. They're going to be furious enough as it is, and we need to get out of here."

"I know that," she said irritably.

"If they catch us now we'll be goners," he insisted.

She couldn't back down now. "I know that, too."

"Other women have disappeared in these mountains and those guys probably had something to do with it," he continued.

"I figured that out after Eric talked about the loss of his latest female companion without a hint of sorrow in his voice," she said in a low voice. "It's just that those idiots who kidnapped me gave me the wrong shoes. They don't fit and I have blisters on top of blisters." She lifted her foot.

Jed cursed violently under his breath. Shelby didn't flinch.

"I'll go as far as I can," she told him. "But I'm afraid to look at my feet and see how bad they are."

Without a word, he grasped her arm and efficiently tossed her over his shoulder. Shelby swallowed her gasp as she found herself looking at his back and a tight pair of buttocks flexing with every step he took.

"Just keep your muscles loose and relaxed," he advised.

Shelby looked around Jed's arm and then wished she hadn't. She'd had no idea they were going virtually straight down. She moaned softly and prayed they would reach safety. She was amazed Jed was so surefooted in the dark, even with the addition of her weight thrown over his shoulder. She prayed he wouldn't slip.

It seemed like hours before Jed abruptly changed direction and moved through heavy brush. In moments, they were in a place that was even darker than outside.

He dipped his shoulder and gently set her on her feet.

Shelby wobbled and grabbed hold of his arm. The ink black darkness didn't allow her to see beyond her nose. The odor made her wish she had lost her sense of smell.

"Just sit here," he told her, helping her to the ground. "I'll be right back."

"Where are you go—" Before she could finish her question she realized she was alone.

Shelby remained seated on the ground, allowing her eyes to adjust to the pitch-black interior. As she sat there, she hoped the slight gamey odor didn't mean they were going to have to share the cave with an animal. When something touched her arm, she almost yelped in fright.

"You could have warned me it was you!" she scolded, feeling her heartbeat triple in pace. "I was ready to scream bloody murder thinking it was a bear. How could you come in so quietly?"

"Being quiet is a habit if you want to stay alive," he said briefly. "I wanted to cover any tracks that might lead to here. I put enough brush across the opening that it might be missed unless they walked right into it." He shrugged off his backpack. A moment later, he flicked on a small lamp that sent out a tiny circle of warm yellow light.

Shelby almost gasped as she looked at Jed. The dark intensity on his face was enough to scare her silly.

"Why are you here?" she asked.

"Why do you think I'm here? You were stupid enough to get taken by two yokels who thought you'd make a great birthday gift for their uncle," he said bluntly, scowling at her. "Someone had to come up here and get you. Your father and I agreed I would be the one."

The comment stung, but she didn't want to fight with him. What she really wanted was for him to gather her in his arms and tell her everything was all right. The thunderclouds that doubled for his eyes told her she shouldn't expect any comfort in the near future.

"Why the hell did you cut your hair?" he asked in a controlled tone.

Shelby had never felt like crying more than she did at that moment. Until a deep streak of anger flared to life, fed by the angry expression on Jed's face.

"I cut it because you liked it long." She used the same controlled voice. "I came up here because I didn't want to see you again. And I ran off with the local version of the "Beverly Hillbillies" because I thought they were going to take me to Vegas. I have never had as much fun as I've had with them!" Her voice rose to a muted shriek. She was so lost in her tirade she didn't notice the tears streaming down her face or the way her lower lip violently trembled. "Does that answer your question?"

But Jed noticed her shocked condition. He reached out and pulled her onto his lap, tucking her head under his chin.

"Hey," he murmured in a low, comforting voice, trailing his hand down her back with slow strokes. "Your hair doesn't look all that bad."

"Oh, stop it!" she sniffed, punching him in the stomach. She muttered a soft curse when she discovered her fist had connected with a surface that felt rock hard. "What's under your T-shirt? A bulletproof vest?" She edged her body as far from his as she could.

"Just me." He knew better than to show any amusement. He belatedly realized she was suffering delayed shock from her kidnapping. "Hey, don't cry. Everything will be fine now."

"How can anything be fine?" She melted into his embrace and curled her arms around his neck. "We're going to have refugees from *Deliverance* coming after us. I can't imagine Eric is going to be happy to find his new housekeeper gone. They have big guns, Jed. They live in the wild. And I wouldn't be surprised if Eric knows martial arts. He has a marine tattoo on his arm!" she wailed at the last.

Jed chuckled softly. "A marine tattoo doesn't mean he knows martial arts. Besides, I wouldn't worry about them."

"That's easy for you to say. You haven't spent time with those smelly creatures." Shelby wrinkled her nose. "I'm positive they didn't believe in taking baths more than twice a year, using a toothbrush or even deodorant! My hair even smells like Chris's cap, and that was awful."

Jed started to say something, then stopped. Shelby stiffened. "What?" she whispered.

He snapped off the light. "I doubt it's them, but let's not take any chances."

Shelby didn't dare breathe as she strained her ears for any out-of-the-ordinary sound. Were the bushes rustling because of a breeze or because someone was walking past them? Was that someone talking under his breath or was her imagination conjuring up the sounds? She didn't want to think the men could have caught up with them so fast. She'd never thought of fear having a taste. Now she knew just how bitter it was.

"Honey, if you keep on tightening your hold you're going to strangle me," Jed murmured in her ear.

She mumbled an apology and immediately loosened her grasp. Jed extricated himself from her grip and made his way to the cave opening.

Shelby held herself still in case any movement could be seen from outside. Now that her vision had adjusted to the dark, she could see the vague outline of Jed's body. She could also see he was holding something. She couldn't believe that was a rifle in his hands, although she'd seen it slung over his shoulder. She couldn't imagine Jed using a gun! She didn't feel relief until he moved back to her.

"Nothing to worry about," he told her as he snapped on the light. "What we heard was rain coming down. This is our lucky break, since we can count on it washing away most traces of our escape."

"Maybe it will erase our trail, but it will also wake them up," she guessed. "And I can't imagine they'll be all that happy about getting wet." By now, she could hear the rain drumming outside.

Jed nodded. "They're going to be even more ticked off when they discover you're gone."

Although the cave was warm, Shelby felt very cold. She wrapped her arms around her body in an effort to get warm, but it didn't do her any good. Jed noticed and reached into his backpack, pulling out a plaid flannel shirt. He draped it around her.

"I can't get warm." She shook her head, confused by her body's sudden drop in temperature.

"Shock," he explained, wrapping the folds of the shirt around her and helping her put her arms through the long sleeves. He carefully rolled up the cuffs. "You've been through a lot. It's natural for you to feel this way."

"No, it's not," she protested between chattering teeth. "I'm always in control. I don't have panic attacks."

"Of course, you don't," he said soothingly, briskly rubbing her arms. "You're a very calm person. But then, you don't get kidnapped every day, either."

"Don't patronize me!" Shelby swatted at him with her hands. She might as well have been batting at a pesky mosquito.

Instead of answering, Jed pulled her into his arms and allowed his body heat to permeate her skin. He remained silent, just keeping his arms around her, with one hand stroking her hair. Shelby might claim she didn't want comfort, but he sensed the best thing he could do for her was offer an unthreatening presence. He hated to think what else those bastards had said to her. It was all too easy to guess. He wondered if they knew just how lucky they were to even be alive.

It wasn't long before Shelby realized she wanted more than comfort from Jed. A strange heat streaked through her veins as her skin felt his against her, a heat intensifying with each slow stroke of his hand against her back. She felt an urge to feel his hands on her bare skin; she wanted to do the same to him. She stealthily moved against his hand the same way a cat might brush against a human hand in hopes of more.

The feel of Jed's hand resting against her bare arm was unbearable. His breath, warm against the back of her neck, sent shock waves to her nerve endings; the rough bristles of his beard electrified her skin. He smelled musky, a healthy tang of sweat coupled with his own scent, which she could have recognized blindfolded.

She muttered incoherently as she twisted in his lap and began tearing at his T-shirt. She grasped the hem and started pulling it upward.

"Shelby." He tried to capture her hands and keep his shirt down.

"No!" she ordered, successfully pulling his shirt up to his neck. "I need you, Jed. I need you *now*."

"You're suffering an adrenaline reaction from what's happened to you," he tried to explain. "It's a natural occurrence after what you've been through. But the way you've been mad at me, you'll only be angrier later on if you go through with this now."

With a strength she had no idea she possessed, she grabbed the back of his head, combing her fingers through the dark, tangled strands. She pulled on his hair until his head bent back. She stared him straight in the eye with a gaze that didn't waver.

"Let me put it to you this way. Those men would have killed me sooner or later," she said succinctly as her other hand fumbled with his jeans' zipper. "For the past two days I've been dragged up a mountain trail that was more rocks and potholes than dirt, threatened with the most disgusting punishments, tied to trees and made to wear a cap that smelled like a skunk that's been dead for a hundred years!" Her voice rose steadily with her agitation. "I have humongous blisters, my skin feels like old leather, and so help me, Jed Hawkins, if you don't make love with me at this very moment I won't be accountable for my actions." By now, she had his zipper lowered and her hand tucked inside the fly. She practically purred with satisfaction when she discovered he wasn't wearing underwear. She curled her fingers around his steely heat.

Jed had no time to reply. He could only react as her hands drew him out and fondled his aroused length and her mouth covered his in an incendiary kiss. Her tongue plunged inside his mouth with the ferocity of a jungle Amazon warrior. This was a woman who was going to take all he could give her—and more.

Shelby didn't want the slow, easy lovemaking they'd shared in the past. Her take-charge manner told him she wanted him without any preliminaries and as hot and wild as he was willing to be. Without taking her mouth away from his, she pushed her pajama bottoms down past her knees and kicked them to one side. With the way Jed was seated on the ground, there was no difficulty in her straddling his lap with her legs hooked around his waist.

"Wait," he said hoarsely, gripping her waist with fingers that held on to her like steel. "I don't have anything with me."

She rested her forehead against his to better gaze into his eyes. Even in the dark, the gray seemed to shimmer like pewter. "If you think I'm going to stop now, you've got another think coming," she said in a raw voice that vibrated with need. "Besides, I'm on the pill."

She slowly lowered herself the rest of the way. When her moist center touched him, Jed was beyond argument. He thrust upward, seating himself inside her with one sure stroke. The moment she felt his heated length slide inside her, she moved with a wild abandon as she sought that pinnacle. Sensing she needed raw power more than gentleness, he thrust upward fast and furiously. She rotated against him in an equally untamed counterpoint, their mouths still fused together and their hands roaming everywhere. Jed propelled his hands under her pajama top to find her breasts. His thumbs flicked her nipples to an aching arousal that shot down through her body, while her hands roamed over his chest as if mapping out every inch of his skin. She raked her fingers over his back as she arched her chest against his. It was as if she was trying to meld her body with his, and with the heat they were generating, it wouldn't have been implausible.

In the back of her mind, Shelby realized Jed was as wild for her as she was for him. Their voracious hunger for each other fueled them as they took and gave, until Shelby finally threw back her head, wanting to scream as the convulsions within her body took over. As if fearing she might be overheard, Jed pulled her face back toward him and captured her mouth with his. They swallowed each other's cries as he pulled her down hard onto his lap while she rotated against him and he thrust upward one last time.

Shelby could feel moisture filming her skin and could taste the salty dampness on Jed's shoulder as she sagged against him. Her chest rose and fell as she forced her respiration back to normal. She couldn't help but notice Jed was having the same problem she was in regaining her breath.

"If I'd known kidnapping would turn you into a wild woman, I would have carried you off long ago," Jed said once he found his voice.

Chapter 6

"This is not like me," Shelby murmured. She felt as if all her bones had melted into a thick pool. The last thing she wanted to do was move. If she did, that meant she'd have to face Jed, and she wasn't sure she was ready for that. She still couldn't believe she had acted in such an abandoned manner. At the moment she wasn't sure whether to be embarrassed at her actions or proud of herself for finding that other side of Jed. He wasn't that self-contained, after all.

"Do you hear me complaining?" There was no mistaking the amusement in his voice.

She carefully eased herself off him and reached for her pajama bottoms. In the end, embarrassment won out. She was positive that her face was a bright red and that her blush went all the way to her toes. She was grateful the darkness in the cave covered her heightened color.

"Shel," Jed said quietly. "You needed to know you were still alive. It's a natural reaction. When you face a dangerous situation and get out of it in one piece, you feel the need to reassure yourself you're still living. I told you that before."

"Yes, but that didn't mean I should practically ravish you," she muttered.

"I did my part, too," he reminded her.

"It's just that Meredith's—" She choked on the name. "All the time they had me I could only think how she was gone and I survived."

He instantly realized what had been tormenting her. "Shelby, Meredith isn't dead."

Her head whipped around, her eyes wide with surprise. "What do you mean she's not dead? I heard her screaming, and when Chris pushed me down the hall I saw her lying on the floor in her bedroom. There was a lot of blood around her head and she wasn't moving. I didn't see her face, but I knew she couldn't be alive."

He shook his head. "She might have been dead if someone from the sheriff's office hadn't gotten right out there to investigate the alarm. He found her and got her to the hospital pronto. There was so much blood because she had a head wound—they always bleed a lot. I visited her in the hospital before I came after you. She has a concussion and some bruises, but she should be out in a few more days. If anything, she's furious at the men for kidnapping you." He smiled. "She told me to get up here and raise some serious hell."

Shelby blinked rapidly, holding back her tears of joy. "I was so upset when I thought they had killed her. And I felt horrible because I knew with her gone, no one would have any idea where I was," she whispered. "Then she was able to give you an idea where they had taken me. That's how you got up here?"

"She was unconscious when they took you," Jed explained. "She didn't know you were kidnapped until after she came to. I took the logical course and started out at her family's cabin before tracking you three up here."

She looked puzzled. "How could you track me? They were making sure to cover any signs we made along the way. They were furious every time I broke even a grass stem."

"They were good at what they did, but I was better," he said without arrogance. "Besides, it's easy enough if you know what kind of signs you're looking for. Some people might have had trouble picking up your trail, but I didn't."

Shelby still couldn't take in all she was hearing. "But you have no experience out here. Or of doing anything like that."

He took a deep breath. "As long as you know which direction is which and find the signs, you don't need familiarity with an area. It was obvious they were taking you up the mountain, so I looked for their tracks and followed them."

"I had no idea you knew anything about the great outdoors," she continued, still trying to puzzle it all out. "After all, when you travel for my father you spend all your time in large cities."

Jed hesitated. "Not always."

Shelby started remembering her father saying things like that—a vague answer that actually said nothing. Suspicion flared up as she mentally went over what Jed had just told her. She felt as if she was adding two plus two but wasn't coming up with four.

"Then where do you go?" she demanded.

"Wherever your father needs me," he said cryptically.

Shelby couldn't believe he could look her in the face and lie to her in such a convincing tone. She was positive something had altered her brain cells over the past couple days; what she ordinarily would have regarded as an unqualified truth she now questioned. She *knew* he was lying. And wondered what else he had lied about.

"Where have you been for the last three months?"

"Hong Kong." He pulled his backpack toward him and rummaged through it. Finding a couple of granola bars, he handed one to her.

Shelby studied the flavors of each bar and reached for his instead. Jed shrugged and tore off the wrapper on the remaining one.

"How do I know you were really in Hong Kong?"

He shot her a lazy smile. "Do you want to see my passport?"

She refused to give in to a smile that usually had her insides melting. "No, because it's easy enough to alter a passport. Instead, for once, I want to hear the truth."

Jed's smile disappeared. "I don't lie to you, Shelby."

"Not even by omission?" She felt as if a few pieces of the puzzle might be starting to fall into place. "I feel as if I've been lied to all my life, Jed."

He bit into his bar and chewed carefully before answering. "Sometimes lies are given because they're easier to handle than the truth."

"Maybe I want to hear the truth." She bit into her own bar and wrinkled her nose as she energetically chewed. "This tastes like dog food."

"It contains all the nutrients a person needs to survive in the wild." He pulled a second bar out and unwrapped it.

"That sounds as if you've eaten a lot of these."

"You know I enjoy a healthy diet," he replied, easily demolishing it.

Shelby reached for the canteen and unscrewed the cap. The water was warm and tasted vaguely metallic, but she didn't care. The moisture was welcome to her dry mouth.

"So do I, but I prefer my food to not only look real but to have some flavor." She nibbled on her bar. "Come to think of it, I can't imagine even a dog eating this."

"There are times when you're grateful for anything edible," he told her.

"Such as?"

He cocked an eyebrow at her seemingly casual question. "When you're hungry."

Shelby thought up several curses she'd like to rain on Jed's head. Where was the soft-spoken man she had dated and made love with all this time? The man she'd always thought walked like a jungle animal but acted like a pussycat, with the manners of an old-fashioned gentleman and a sex drive guaranteed to send any woman wild? She always thought of him as the best of two worlds. She remembered once hearing a man saying he wanted a woman who was a lady in public and a courtesan in private. Switch the gender and she felt that described Jed perfectly.

She had told Meredith she wished Jed would lose his control and break out of that shell. She feared he'd done just that.

"I'm very tired," she murmured, pulling his flannel shirt closer around her. She edged back to the cave wall and started to lie down, but Jed stopped her.

"We need to get your feet taken care of," he told her. "Can't afford having those blisters get infected."

"And I suppose you have a first-aid kit in that bottomless pit of a backpack," she said sarcastically.

"It's always a good idea to have one when you're out somewhere like this." He pulled out a metal container and opened it. Within moments, he had bandages, antiseptic, a small bottle of alcohol and gauze pads laid out. He took off one shoe with great care, but she still couldn't prevent her groan of pain as the raw skin on the ball of her foot met the air.

Jed winced as he studied the angry-looking flesh. "I'm afraid no matter how careful I am, this is going to hurt," he warned.

She gritted her teeth in preparation. "Go for it."

Shelby hissed what could have been a curse or a prayer as Jed's sensitive fingers cleaned the blisters, then covered them with gauze pads and wound a bandage around her foot. After he finished he turned his attention to her other foot.

"We're going to have to keep those as clean and dry as possible," he told her as he rummaged through his backpack again. He pulled out a pair of white socks and handed them to her. "These should help some."

Shelby nodded as she slid the heavy cotton over her feet. They were too big but felt like heaven to her abused feet.

Jed also pulled a metallic blanket out of his backpack and handed it to her.

She hesitated before taking it from him. "What will you use?" She was not going to suggest they share the blanket.

"I think I'll stay awake awhile," he told her. "I want to make sure we don't receive any unwanted visitors."

Her eyes widened in alarm. "Even with the rain?"

"They're not going to get you again, Shelby," he assured her.

Even in the dim light, she could see how tired he was. "How long have you been back?" she asked softly.

He shrugged. "A little over two days."

"What about sleep?"

"I'm used to going without sleep."

Shelby's alarm intensified when she saw him pull a gun from the back of his jeans—she couldn't believe she hadn't noticed it when they made love—and set it down in front of him. He slipped a nasty-looking knife out of his boot and placed it next to the rifle. She gulped. He glanced up and caught her expression. A tiny smile tipped up the corners of his lips.

"What did you think I'd do if they showed up, sweetheart? Bargain with them for your charms? Tell them they were bad boys, but if they went away quietly, we'd all forget about it?"

She winced, realizing she could easily have thought just that. "But guns are dangerous," she said inanely.

"Only if you don't know how to use them."

Shelby felt as if she had one other tidbit to add to the growing list of details she was compiling on Jed. She clutched the blanket in front of her. "Did I ever know the real you?"

The soft pain in her voice reached out to Jed, but he forced his feelings back to that dark place deep inside him. She had rejected him once, he reminded himself. If she knew the entire truth, she'd only reject him again.

"Nowadays a person can't be too careful," he said flippantly. "Why don't you get some rest, Shelby? You'll feel better in the morning."

She curled up in a ball, dragging the blanket over her. "Only if there's coffee and a hot shower waiting," she murmured before rolling over, presenting her back to him. "Leave a late wake-up call with the operator, please."

Jed looked at the expanse of tousled, fiery hair. She said she had cut it because of him. She knew how much he enjoyed seeing her hair flowing down her back and across her naked breasts when they made love. Had those memories tormented her that much?

He settled back against the opposite wall of the cave, where he had a clear view out and an equally advantageous view of Shelby's back. The soft sound of her breathing as she slept reached his sharp ears, as did the trickle of rain dripping off the rocks. They seemed to him to be lonely sounds. Just as lonely as he suddenly felt.

* * *

"When I find that bitch and whoever helped her get away, I'm going to skin them both." Chris's coarse voice floated through the cave opening.

Jed stiffened and reached for his rifle. He looked across the cave and noticed that Shelby's eyes were open. She looked apprehensive but didn't say a word or move a muscle. She kept her gaze trained on him as she lay stiffly under the blanket. He couldn't keep his eyes off her as his mind ran through various plans of action.

"Maybe they got all the way down." It was Andy's voice.

"With all this rain?" Eric snarled. "You look over that way. There's a cluster of trees that makes a natural umbrella. They could be hiding there. Don't go charging in like a herd of elephants. Whoever's with her might have a gun. I'm gonna look in the other direction." As he walked away, he graphically described what he'd do to Shelby once he found her, what would happen to the bastard who'd freed her and what would happen to Andy and Chris for letting her escape if she wasn't found.

Jed hated that Shelby had to hear Eric's tirade. What he said didn't surprise Jed. He sensed the man had seen the military as his life and war as his sustenance. When there wasn't a war for him to fight, he must have had no idea how to function. Like others, he'd retreated to the mountains where he could live the way he felt he was meant to—off the land. Jed also had an idea that if Sheriff Rainey went back further in his files, he'd find more reports of women disappearing. Jed had seen enough of Eric to know the man had lost his handle on reality a long time ago.

Jed looked across the dim interior at Shelby, sitting against the wall. He was pleased that she hadn't moved a muscle, although her expression changed as she listened to Eric's description of what he wanted to do to her. Jed wanted to assure her that Eric wouldn't get a chance to touch even a strand of her hair. The men's voices finally receded as they moved farther down the mountain and Jed breathed a silent sigh of relief. As soon as he felt it was safe enough, he crawled across the cave until he was sitting cross-legged next to her.

"They still might come back this way in hopes we'll get overconfident and give ourselves away," he said in a voice that wouldn't travel any farther than her ears. "He thinks he's dealing with amateurs."

"Little does he know," she murmured.

Shelby sat quietly, allowing her senses to reach out. The gamey aroma in the cave hadn't receded, but she could also detect the musky scent of Jed's skin, the barely muted sound of his breathing, the rustle of bushes outside as the breeze moved through them. The longer she sat, the more she imagined she could hear Eric furiously ordering his nephews to just shut up and look for clues.

It seemed like hours before Jed moved.

"Old Uncle Eric seems to have a one-track mind," he murmured.

Shelby grimaced. "And unfortunately, I seem to be the prey this time." She stretched her legs out in front of her, then bent at the waist, touching her toes. She could feel the faint pull in her legs as stiff muscles started to stretch and relax. "Why doesn't he just give up and send his idiot nephews out for another woman?"

"He doesn't appreciate that you got away from him," Jed explained. "He also doesn't want anyone knowing he's the one taking women."

"What makes him think I couldn't get away on my own?" She sounded disgruntled as she stretched one arm over her head, then the other arm.

Jed smiled at that. "You forget he's from another era, when women wouldn't have had the courage to escape on their own. He figures you couldn't survive out here alone. No offense, but someone who looks like you usually can't take more than two steps without screaming because a bug crawled across her feet."

Shelby's eyes dropped to her feet, then to the cave floor. Jed chuckled. "See what I mean?"

She resisted the urge to scratch her back. Now that she thought of it, she did wonder if that itch along her spine might be due to a creepy-crawly.

"Women are very resourceful and he should realize it," she grumbled.

"Do you want to be the one to educate him?"

Shelby wrinkled her nose in disgust. "I'd rather eat mud." She took a deep breath. "Speaking of mud, do you have any more of those granola bars?"

Jed pulled a couple out of his backpack and dropped one in her lap.

"There's a stream not far from here. I'll go out later and fill the canteen," he told her.

"How long will we have to stay here?"

"I'd like to wait until tomorrow. By then they might have given up and returned to their cabin."

"But they also might not have," she concluded. "They took a big risk kidnapping me. I can't imagine they'll give me up all that easily." She toyed with her shirt buttons. "You're right, they don't have a good grip on reality. None of them do. I guess it's all that clean air up here. Their lungs can't handle it." She chuckled, then burst out laughing. "Isn't it funny, Jed? That it's the clean air that makes people crazy, not the smog?" She giggled so hard she started to choke.

Jed grasped her shoulders and shook her hard. "Stop it!" he ordered. "Shelby, you've got to snap out of it."

Her head bobbed back and forth. It took her a moment but she swallowed the sobbing laughter that kept bubbling up. "I can't imagine why I ever thought I led an uneventful life," she said once she'd regained her breath. She took several deep breaths. "I don't suppose you have a deck of cards in that bottomless pit, do you?"

He shook his head. "Sorry."

"A good book?"

He shook his head again. "All I cared about was reaching you and getting you back down the mountain. I didn't expect I'd have to entertain you, too."

Shelby leaned back against the wall. "Since it appears you do have to entertain me, you may as well start off by telling me the truth. What exactly do you do for my father?"

"You already know."

"I don't think so." She examined her nails, grimacing when she noted broken ends and chipped polish. "My manicurist is going to have a fit when she sees these nails." She turned her head so she could look at him. "I'm seeing you in a much different light up here."

"Oh? In what way?" He didn't appear concerned that she was trying to dissect him.

Shelby shifted her body so that she leaned sideways against the wall. "The Jed Hawkins I know wouldn't have had any idea how to track those men. He would have hired someone experienced in tracking and come up with him, perhaps, but not gone on his own. The Jed I know wouldn't handle guns and knives so familiarly, either. Or while tracking us, manage to find a few hideaways at the same time."

Jed still didn't appear fazed by her observations. "When you travel overseas as much as I do, you learn to use a weapon and carry one for protection."

She held up her hand. "That's another thing. I call it a gun. You call it a weapon."

He shrugged. "Means the same thing."

Shelby shook her head. "I remember hearing that people in law enforcement or any field like that call a gun a weapon just as you do." She leaned forward slightly. "I always ignored my father's habit of keeping secrets. But I'm remembering things now that are bringing up a lot of questions."

He looked at her warily. "Such as?"

"Such as the windows in all his cars having bulletproof glass. Such as my being driven to school every day. Now that I think of it, the driver always carried a gun." She ticked the items off on her fingers. "Such as all the times Daddy took trips the way you do now. Such as the time he was hospitalized and claimed it was emergency surgery. Such as I've never truly gone to his office. Oh, he's taken me to the place he calls his office, but now that I think about it, I realize it didn't feel like one.''

"And what does an office feel like?" Jed asked.

"As if someone really does work there." She paused. "Your office felt the same way. That building is tall, more than twenty-five floors. I'd say your real office is somewhere else in it. Perhaps it's on one of those floors that require a key card and palm print to get off on."

Jed grew still. "How do you know about that?"

"It's easy when you try to go up to a certain floor and the elevator won't stop there," she replied. "My father is also on speaking terms with a great many higher-ups in the government. A mere owner of an import/export firm wouldn't know so many of them."

"One would if he does a lot of business with them, and I wouldn't call your father a mere owner," he countered easily. "You know Warren moves freely in Washington, D.C., circles."

She shook her head. "It's too pat. I've read too many spy novels where an import/export firm was a front for—" She stopped abruptly as the truth hit her.

At the same time Jed said, "Don't get your imagination working overtime now."

"Spies," she murmured. She lifted her face. "Yes, I can see it. The travel, the secrecy, the way Daddy cut himself off from having another relationship after Mom died even though he knew I wouldn't have minded if he found someone else. The way you've always kept to yourself." Her smile held a hint of sorrow. "Oh, I used to hear a lot about you. How you'd break my heart. That you couldn't commit to anyone. But considering what you really do for a living, it's understandable you wouldn't want anyone too close to you. The enemy would see that as a weakness and go after that person instead. Not to mention you have an apartment that could easily double for a hotel suite—there isn't one hint of you anywhere to be found. Nothing that could give you away. Am I right, Jed? Do you and my father work for the government?"

He silently cursed the twists and turns of her quick mind. "You've seen too many James Bond films."

"I must admit you wear a tuxedo as well as he does," she said, tongue in cheek.

He sliced a searing glance in her direction. "I don't remember this smart mouth of yours."

She lifted her chin and flashed him a smile worthy of a duchess. "It appeared about the same time as Chris and Andy."

"Then logically, it should have left with them," Jed muttered.

"But I'm a woman," she cooed, offering him that same smile. "I don't have to be logical."

His reply was blunt and to the point.

Shelby rolled her eyes. "Typical male response. Listen, buster." She poked him in the chest with her forefinger.

Buster? Jed cocked an eyebrow.

She ignored his expression and went on. "A lot has happened since you flew off into the wild blue yonder."

"That's the air force," he murmured.

She shot him a quelling look. "What I'm saying is I took stock of our relationship and decided the best thing that ever happened was our breaking up."

"We didn't break up," he grunted, not liking this conversation at all.

"Yes, we did," she stated.

"*You* said it was over. *I* told you we would discuss it when we got back." Only with willpower was he able to keep his voice low.

"And *I* told you there was nothing more to discuss," Shelby retorted. "What I'm trying to explain is I realized I didn't like the person I was turning into. I decided the best thing I could do was have a life of my own."

"You have a life of your own," he argued. "What about your personal shopping service? Not to mention you serve on a couple of charity boards."

"Yes, but I still allowed my life to revolve around you," she noted. "I realized that was a big mistake and decided I would take back my life. My first step was going to the cabin with Meredith."

"Which didn't turn out all that well," he murmured.

She crossed her arms in front of her chest. "Not my fault. And it's not an experience I intend to repeat."

"I'll make sure of that."

As Jed's words sunk in, Shelby glared at him. "Wait a minute. You're trying to get me off the subject, aren't you?" she said accusingly. "I'd rather you tell me the truth instead, Jed. Are you or aren't you a spy?"

Most people would grow uneasy under Jed's silent regard. Shelby merely waited patiently, her arms still crossed in front of her.

"I believe the correct term would be government agent."

She tapped her fingers against the opposite arm. "I gather *our* government?"

He exhaled a breath of frustration. "Yes, our government, dammit! Why can't you ever take what I say and just let it be?"

Chapter 7

Shelby's eyes gleamed with anger. "I should have known there was something odd going on. Why didn't I see it?" She threw up her hands. "How could I have missed something this important?"

"It's not something we care to advertise to the public," Jed said from between clenched teeth.

She turned on him with the ferocity of a cornered wildcat. "I am not the public," she coldly informed him. "This is not a secret a man should keep from his own daughter."

"It's safer for all involved if you don't know all the particulars," he said. "Your father's position and my own require a very high security clearance. We are frequently involved with sensitive issues. The fewer outsiders who know about us and what we do, the safer they'll be."

Shelby wasn't sure whether to be frustrated by his words or sad that people were forced to live such clandestine lives.

"Then why wasn't I at least told you worked for the government? What harm would there have been in saying that? All you had to do was allow me to think you were some kind of courier or attaché. Wouldn't that have been kinder than saying absolutely nothing? And why use an import/export firm as a front?" She shook her head as she tried to assimilate all she'd learned so far.

"The firm is legitimate. Thanks to having the company, we've been able to make some excellent contacts in Southeast Asia and South America that have proven useful at times," Jed explained. "Traveling there on a buying trip looks better than saying we're going in for other reasons."

"What kind of reasons?"

He shook his head. "You don't need to know that."

"Why am I not surprised?" she said wryly. "Fine, so when you were gone, it wasn't to check out the offices or look into a special purchase, was it?" she asked, undeterred by his continued silence. "You had another reason for your trips, didn't you?"

Jed shook his head again. "No more, Shelby. It's up to your father to tell you what he wants you to know."

"Which means he won't tell me anything." Shelby sat back. "I imagine he was very upset to hear about my abduction."

Jed thought of the gray-faced man lying in the hospital bed. He imagined he could hear the soft whooshes of the ventilator hooked up to the older man. He'd already decided not to tell Shelby about Warren's heart attack until they were off the mountain. He figured she had enough to worry about thanks to Eric, Chris and Andy.

"He was," he said in a clipped tone.

She had a sudden horrifying thought. "Did he think my kidnapping had something to do with what he does?"

He shook his head. "He knew there was no chance of that happening."

She sat back, frustrated at hearing so much and yet learning so little. She suddenly perked up as another thought occurred to her. "Did you bring your cell phone with you? We could call Daddy to tell him I'm all right, and then we could call the local sheriff to come up and get those creeps."

He shook his head. "I left it back in the car. There was no guarantee we could transmit with all the mountains around us, and as it is I wouldn't count on any help from the local law. Sheriff Rainey is only interested in keeping tourism alive in his happy little town, which means keeping these guys out of the public attention."

"I gather you made a good impression on the sheriff," Shelby murmured, not missing the disgust in his voice. She had to admit she wasn't feeling very charitable toward the lawman just now.

"Let's just say he's lucky he's still in one piece."

Shelby shifted her position and tucked her legs under her body. "I guess I'll have to wait until we're back down before I can call home." She glanced over her shoulder at the cave opening. "Is there any chance

I could sneak out there for a quick trip to the bushes?'' she asked hopefully.

He nodded. ''It should be safe enough. I'll keep a lookout.''

She stood up and tied the shirttails at her waist as she walked toward the cave opening.

''Oh, Shelby?''

She turned around.

Jed was grinning broadly. ''Make sure I see the top of your head.''

Shelby's reply was silent, but her upraised finger told him how she felt about his quip. Jed's low chuckle followed her out.

She would have preferred to spend more time outside, breathing in the crisp, clean air that still held a hint of rain, but she knew she couldn't take any chances. As it was, she still felt Chris's slimy hands on her skin. He had enjoyed touching her all too much during their trek. She rubbed her arms briskly, wishing fervently for a long hot bath.

Even with Jed as lookout, Shelby couldn't help but peer over her shoulder every few seconds as if she feared Eric or Chris would suddenly jump out of the bushes. She spooked herself so thoroughly that she scurried back into the cave, with Jed following at a more leisurely pace.

''I just want to go home,'' she moaned, dropping down onto the dirt floor. ''I want to get away from here before Eric and his idiotic nephews show up. I want to see for myself that Meredith is all right. I want to hug my father and promise him I'll never worry him again.'' She looked up, forlorn as a child. ''I want to sleep in my own bed.''

Jed sat down beside her and wrapped his arms around her, pulling her onto his lap. "We'll leave tomorrow," he promised her.

"I wished you'd brought your cell phone with you or even some other kind of radio," she said, laying her cheek against his chest. "Don't spies—correction, government agents—have wrist radios or something so they can check in with their control officer or whatever?"

His chest rose and fell under her cheek. "This is not a subject open for discussion."

"Then Daddy should have told me the truth about himself." Her forehead furrowed in thought. "I don't think I want any more surprises. I've had more than enough, thank you." She straightened up. "Actually, by rights, I shouldn't be talking to you."

"Perhaps I want to talk to you." He ran his hand down her hair, grimacing when he realized it reached the ends a lot sooner than it used to. "I told you before I left that we needed to talk. Now's as good a time as any." Especially when he feared she'd take off for parts unknown the moment he got her back to L.A.

"When you got back were you going to tell me what you really did for a living?" she asked.

"No."

His low-voiced reply was expected but still hurt. What pained Shelby even more was the absence of regret in his answer. She straightened and would have slid off his lap, but his arms refused to release her.

"What were you going to tell me then?"

Jed rested his chin on top of her head. "I would have reminded you how good we are together. And not just the sex, either." He tapped her nose when he saw her mouth open with the expected retort. "We never lacked for conversation when we went out. We have similar taste in foods, music and films. We enjoy a lot of the same sports."

"I wasn't trying to trap you, Jed." Shelby spoke hastily, before he could interrupt her again. "I just felt we were coming to a fork in the road in our relationship and I didn't want to see us as nothing more than a long-term affair. I didn't want to think that the day would come when you wouldn't call because you'd found someone else and you didn't have the courage to tell me so."

Jed whipped her around to face him. His face was dark with anger. "When I am with one woman, I stay with that woman," he said fiercely. "I have never been unfaithful to you. And if you want facts and figures, I hadn't been with anyone for almost a year before I met you."

"Jed, I trust you." Her tone gentled. "No man is more honorable than you are. But I feel so uncertain about what's between us."

"A piece of paper doesn't mean a damn thing, nor do words spoken because two parties feel they're necessary," Jed said between gritted teeth.

This time Shelby had no problem slipping off his lap. She already felt the loss of his body against hers. Judging by the stormy lights in Jed's eyes, they were headed for a full-fledged battle.

After that night she had left Jed in his apartment, she sensed he might have pressured her to come back to him, but it would have been on his terms. Other men had asked her to marry them and she had declined because she hadn't felt anything for them. Now the one man she wanted to marry was in her life, and while he wanted to spend time with her and make love with her, he didn't want to make a commitment to her. At the moment she wasn't sure whether to throw something at him or cry. She kept her back to him and walked over to his pack.

"I want to start down today."

Jed narrowed his eyes at her wooden tone. "It's too soon."

"I don't care. If you won't take me back now I'll go by myself. It can't be all that difficult. All I have to do is go down." She refused to look at him.

He felt a twisting sensation deep in his gut. It was just like that night. She wouldn't look at him and she wanted nothing to do with him. He wondered what she'd say if he told her he'd expected this behavior. This was why he never committed himself to anyone—so there was no worry about being left behind later on.

And Shelby *would* leave him behind. Her life-style dictated it. She was made for traveling the world in a much different manner than he did. While she visited opulent resorts, he was usually traveling through a steamy jungle or an occasional arid desert. She had already intimated she wasn't too happy to hear the truth about his occupation. Soon she would realize the last thing she needed in her life was a man who could kill without leaving a trace.

Jed knew he cared for Shelby more than he had ever cared for any woman. He thought he had gotten that fact across to her. Not in words, but in the way he worshipped her with his body. What did he have to do to prove himself to her? Give her words that really didn't mean anything?

Until he saw her flinch he hadn't realized he'd said it aloud.

Shelby sat down and dragged the shoes over the socks. She winced when she stood up, but managed to walk without limping as she headed for the cave opening.

"I'll get down myself," she said just as she disappeared out the opening.

Jed muttered a curse as he jumped to his feet. He gathered up his weapons and the backpack and followed within seconds.

As he started down the mountain he was gratified to see she wasn't taking the regular trail but making her own path paralleling it. She didn't turn around when he caught up to her.

"You can't do this by yourself."

She kept her eyes straight ahead. "Sure I can."

He grabbed her arm and spun her around, then winced when her fist connected with his midriff. Jed's mouth opened and closed as he fought to catch his breath.

"Damn!" Shelby shook her hand. "I think I broke my hand."

"Don't expect any sympathy from me," he wheezed. "What are you trying to do?"

She placed her hands on her hips. "Go to hell." She spun on one heel and marched off.

"Damn woman," he muttered, taking off after her.

Jed kept all his senses working overtime as he looked and listened for any sign that they had been spotted. Considering the heavy foliage around them, he feared the men could creep up on them unde-tected.

"More and more I'm wondering if you're worth all this trouble," he grumbled, walking past her and taking the lead.

"More and more I'm wishing you'd remained wherever you were," she retorted, although she made sure not to speak too loudly.

Jed turned around so swiftly that Shelby was forced to back up a couple steps. The fury etched on his face made her step back another pace.

"You ought to be damn glad I showed up when I did," he told her in a low voice that fairly vibrated with anger. "Do you have any idea what those men had in store for you?"

"Housekeeping, cooking, probably chopping some wood and hauling water in from the stream along with sharing good ol' Uncle Eric's bed," she re-torted, sticking her chin out.

"And when he got tired of you you'd be passed on to the nephews as a new toy," Jed told her. "I think you can guess which nephew would have you next. That bastard was ready to tear your clothes off and dive into that luscious body of yours. He was so hot and bothered I'm amazed he didn't turn to steam." Jed's eyes raked her figure. "I'm not surprised, con-sidering what you have on."

Shelby's eyes narrowed to glowing emerald slits. "Well, pardon me all to hell," she drawled sarcasti-cally. "If I had known I was going to be pulled out of bed in the middle of the night and dragged halfway up a mountain I would have made sure to wear something more suitable. Khakis and hiking boots, for instance.''

Jed bit down on any further comments he was tempted to make. "The last thing we need to do is fight while we're out here in the open," he muttered, spearing his fingers through his hair. The dark locks hung loosely around his shoulders, making him look like the barbarian he felt. A streak of dirt on his cheek and the tear in his jeans and another in his T-shirt furthered the renegade picture he affected without even trying.

He took a deep breath. What would it take for her to understand? He couldn't remember ever feeling so frustrated about one person. Not sexually frustrated—if he didn't know any better he'd swear it was a frustration of his emotions. No woman had ever caused the internal turmoil that Shelby had created inside him from the first time he saw her.

"Let's just get down this damn mountain," he growled.

Shelby refused to utter one word of complaint as they made their way down. She was positive Jed had deliberately chosen a difficult route as she picked her way around rocks and moved through brush that snagged at her clothing. She was grateful for the protection his shirt gave her as she again stopped to pull a branch from her hair. Her eyes stung from the pain to her scalp but she decided it was a necessary evil.

How come his hair doesn't get tangled up in bushes and trees? she wondered, casting murderous glares at Jed's back. *He doesn't trip over rocks, he walks like a damn mountain goat and he never has to stop.* She stumbled to a halt and bent over, bracing her hands on her knees. "Excuse me, Kit Carson, but going downhill isn't turning out to be as easy as going uphill." She sat down on a rock.

Jed turned around and walked back to her. "We can't spend a lot of time working on our tans," he warned her.

Shelby looked skyward. "Where did this sarcastic side of Jed Hawkins come from?" she asked no one in particular. "I remember this soft-spoken, gentle man with an intense side, but I don't recall Mr. Macho or Mr. Sarcasm." She turned her head to stare daggers at Jed. "Are you sure you don't have an identical twin? One good, one bad and I'm just unlucky enough to be stuck with the bad one this time?"

"Why are you trying to tick me off?" he asked in a dangerously soft voice.

"Why are you acting like James Bond on a bad day?" she countered. She sat back, entranced by the dark red color washing his cheekbones. She suddenly felt that wicked excitement of walking a tightrope without a safety net. There was no doubt she was pushing him . . . hard. And he didn't like it.

"Get off your bottom and move those feet," he ordered in that same low, dangerous tone. "As it is, I'm going to need to find us a hiding place tonight."

She straightened up at that piece of news. "Tonight? What do you mean, tonight? We should be down the mountain by tonight."

"We're taking a more circular route for safety's sake, which is going to take us longer," he said a bit impatiently. "Not to mention we're moving at a slower pace."

"Slower?" she echoed. "We're going downhill! We should be able to go faster downhill than uphill! I itch, Jed! I'm positive there are bugs nesting in my clothes and hair! My teeth feel as if there's sand all over them and I'm so dirty I don't think I'll ever get clean!"

Jed grabbed her hand and pulled her upright. He used his other hand to grasp the back of her head and hold it still for his kiss, which literally took her breath away. When he pulled back, she was breathing hard and looked glassy eyed. "Then let's head downhill." He walked swiftly, still hanging on to her hand.

Shelby had no choice but to keep up if she didn't want her shoulder dislocated.

"Once upon a time you were a really nice guy," she gasped.

He quickened his steps, as if he didn't appreciate her remark. "Yeah, well, sweetheart, you can forget about it. From now on there's no more Mister Nice Guy," he practically snarled.

Chapter 8

Shelby told herself to be grateful that Jed had found a fairly comfortable hiding place for the night, even if it wasn't a cave but a shelf of rocks that hid them from view of anyone who might be walking on one of the regular trails.

"No light tonight, I'm afraid," he apologized once they were settled on the rocky shelf. "We can't afford for anyone to see it."

"Maybe we'll have a full moon tonight," she said with a hopeful smile.

"Not tonight." He pulled out granola bars and handed her one. "There's no moon, which is in our favor." He noted her expression of distaste as she stared at the bar. "It's guaranteed to up your energy level, and you're going to need all the strength you can get if you want to be down by tomorrow night."

She wrinkled her nose as she nibbled on her dinner. "It may advertise it gives you plenty of energy, but I, for one, can vouch that it tastes like dirt."

Jed chuckled. "I thought you said it tasted like dog food."

She was undeterred. "I'm sure dog food tastes like dirt, too. No wonder I preferred to pass on the outdoor life." Shelby finished her small meal in record time and sat back, curling her legs under her as she looked down. "Any other time I probably would have thought this was beautiful. I had no idea just how dangerous it could be."

"Before, you were on the outskirts. That cabin overlooks a lake on one side and forest on the other," he said, following the direction of her gaze. "But inside you had all the comforts of home, and a car to whisk you to civilization. It's easy to forget just how dangerous it can be out here. Oh, you might hear a news story about a mountain lion appearing too close to town or a bear attacking, but it always happens to someone else. You forget just how easily it can happen to you."

"Except my enemy was man," she murmured. "Do you think the sheriff will be able to track them down and bring them in?"

Jed didn't want to burst her hopeful bubble, but he didn't want her to relax her guard, either. He didn't plan to relax his. He wasn't going to tell her that he intended to offer to lead a party of men back up here to find Eric and his nephews and bring them in. He wanted Shelby to be the last woman they seized for their own use.

Shelby shifted her position, drawing her knees up under her chin and looping her arms around her drawn-up legs. She looked down at the green expanse of leafy trees and brush spread out before her. She inhaled the sharp tang of pine into her lungs. She continued looking down because it was easier than looking at Jed. Every time she did, she only felt pain. Their walk had helped her work her anger out of her system. Now she just felt hurt that he had chosen to keep his true occupation a secret. She felt that same pain realizing her father had done the same, but Jed was here and Warren wasn't.

"Would you ever have told me what you really did for a living?"

Jed couldn't miss the anguish in her voice. He only wished he had the right answer to give her. "Probably not."

"Because you decided the day would come when we would part company and it would be better I didn't know?" she asked. "Or perhaps you'd end up shot or dead during one of your assignments or missions or whatever you call them and again, it wouldn't matter?" She turned her head so she could face him. "What would be the explanation given back here? You were robbed at gunpoint? Airplane or taxi accident? How is it handled?"

He felt uneasy at Shelby's all too casually voiced question. "It depends on the circumstances."

"What circumstances?"

For lack of something better to do, he placed his rifle on the ground next to his knife.

"What circumstances, Jed?" she repeated.

"Whether the agent has any family or not," he murmured. He ignored the strange twisting feeling in the pit of his stomach.

She continued looking at him steadily. "If there is a family?"

He took a deep breath. "Nine times out of ten, the family doesn't know what kind of work the agent is involved in. They're notified that there was a fatal accident and they're taken care of by the agency from then on."

"And if the agent has no family?" she whispered. "What happens then?"

Jed still didn't look at Shelby. He recalled a man he'd partnered with many times over the years. A man with no family, no close ties to anyone.

Jed had been the only one present at the memorial service before his partner's ashes were scattered to the wind. To this day, Jed was positive he was the only one to mourn the passing of a fine individual.

"The body is cremated and the ashes scattered," he said with absolutely no emotion in his voice. For all anyone knew, he could have been talking about the weather.

Shelby was so quiet he wondered if she had heard him. He finally turned to meet her gaze. And he wished he hadn't. The pity shining from her eyes made him want to lash out at her.

"How sad that anyone would not be mourned and remembered for the good they did," she whispered. "No one should be forgotten in such a callous way."

"You forget." He spoke more roughly than he intended; he was still smarting from what he read in her eyes. "Your father has you to mourn him."

"Who will mourn you, Jed?" Her soft voice washed over him like liquid satin. "Will I be relegated to overhearing of your demise in casual conversation and learning that your ashes were scattered to the winds with no one there? Who will remember you?"

His eyes flashed with fury—a fury he hated feeling because it showed just how vulnerable he was to her.

"I'll be dead. It won't matter that there won't be anyone to care," he said in a harsh voice meant to lacerate.

She didn't change her expression. "Oh, I think it will matter much more than you realize."

Unwilling to look at Shelby any longer, Jed pushed himself to his feet.

"I'm going to make sure our tracks are covered and that our friends aren't anywhere close by," he muttered before taking off. "Don't go off by yourself before I get back or make too many movements. Sound carries a far distance out here."

She didn't say a word, only watched him leave.

Shelby remained in her drawn-up position as she mulled over her conflicting emotions. She had just viewed yet another facet of Jed. After the cold, calculating male animal, she was surprised to see this vulnerable side. She could sense he didn't like showing this part of his personality any more than he enjoyed showing his harsher side.

She thought of the scars she had seen on his body—scars he had explained away as boyhood accidents or muggings during his travels. She'd once even teased him that he shouldn't travel if he was so unlucky with local thugs. He'd merely smiled. Now she knew why he found her teasing amusing.

She realized she had been too willing to accept his glib explanations because she hadn't wanted to look any deeper into the man himself. He had always been the perfect escort, the perfect partner for social functions and most definitely the perfect lover. Because she hadn't wanted to open her eyes to reality, she'd allowed herself to be blinded. Even when she had decided she wanted more from him, she hadn't thought any further than his giving her that all-important commitment of himself.

Jed hadn't lied to her; he just avoided giving her the truth. Technically, her father hadn't lied to her, either. That was something else she vowed to rectify as soon as she got home. She intended to sit the man down and insist he tell her everything, no matter how hard he resisted. She didn't want any more secrets between them.

She looked out but didn't see a sign of Jed. She didn't expect to. If she couldn't detect even a hint of his dark clothing or hear a rustle in the brush, then Eric wouldn't, either. It was obvious Jed was very good at what he did, but she had to remind herself he had to be better than good if he wanted to remain alive.

"All I wanted to do was get away from him," she told herself under her breath. "I thought coming out here would free me of all I felt for him. Instead, all it did was bind me even closer to the man."

She thought of the wild lovemaking they'd shared back in the cave and blushed at the memory of the way she'd practically ordered him to possess her. She

had almost torn his clothing off his body in her eagerness to make love with him! The more she recalled that night, the higher her body temperature
rose. Had she really said and done all those things?
Not to mention the almost raw savagery he'd shown
in response. She decided there was a lot more to Jed
than she was aware of, and in one respect, at least, she
certainly wouldn't mind finding out what!

Shelby fumbled for the canteen. She splashed a little water onto her hands so she could pat her heated
cheeks, but found it didn't cool her off any.

"At this rate, I don't think even an ice-cold shower
would work," she muttered, sipping some water. She
sat back on the shelf so as to remain out of sight and
prepared to wait for Jed's return.

Jed didn't like what he was finding. Someone less
cynical and suspicious than he was would think the
three men were walking in circles. But Jed knew better. The men were still looking for them and were
beating the bushes, making tight circles so they
wouldn't miss the smallest hiding place. Jed was positive they were deliberately not hiding their tracks.
They wanted him to know they weren't going to give
up. That was fine with him, since he could keep track
of them at the same time.

He rubbed his palm over his jaw, grimacing at the
bristles prickling his skin.

"Damn, it could take us an extra day to avoid running into them," he murmured. His mouth twisted in
a wry smile. "By then we're both going to wish I'd
brought more than those blasted granola bars."

Jed made no sound as he made his way back to the
rocky shelf. Shelby was seated on the camp blanket
with the ends tucked securely around her feet. His
shirt was still wrapped around her, although it was
already the worse for wear. Her eyes were shadowed
with fatigue and the bruise on her cheek was turning
an interesting shade of yellow-green.

"Did you see them?" she asked as he dropped
down beside her.

He looked down on her serene features and silently damned her well-bred demeanor, which revealed no sign of emotion. He found he preferred the
fiery, passionate side he'd seen last night. He vowed
he'd see it again.

He shook his head. He wasn't about to hide the
truth from her anymore. "But they're taking a cir-
cuitous route in hopes of catching us unaware along
the way."

Only a slight tensing of her lips told him she was
uneasy at his news. "Which means?"

"They don't know what training I've had or what
I have at my disposal. They do know there's only one
person to deal with, and they're thinking I'm just an
amateur who got lucky," he said bluntly. "Which
means if they can, they'll shoot to kill."

Shelby jumped as if a loud noise had startled her.
"Punishment for your taking me from them," she
murmured.

"They don't want us getting down the mountain
where we can give the authorities an excellent description of them and provide a rough idea where
they're living," he explained. "Their fun and games
up here would be rudely interrupted."

"No one knows what they might have up there by way of protection," Shelby said. "For all we know, they could have their front yard littered with land mines."

"It would be a good way to keep solicitors away," Jed commented with a wry smile.

Shelby smiled back. "Better than a large dog."

"Cheaper, too." His smile disappeared. "Do you know how to shoot?"

Her eyes widened as she realized his intent. "Daddy didn't like having a gun in the house. At least, that's what he used to say. Now I'm wondering if he didn't have one hidden somewhere."

"I'm sure he did." Jed picked up his rifle and proceeded to show her what she needed to know to protect herself. Basically, all he cared about was that she aim and shoot. "The ammunition this baby is carrying is considered illegal by some, but it's guaranteed to do more than enough damage as long as you hit your target. Don't stop there. Just keep shooting. All I ask is that you make sure not to shoot me." He handed her the rifle. "Also be prepared for a kick that could knock you on your lovely butt."

She accepted the weapon gingerly. She started to lay it in her lap, then changed her mind and placed it in front of her. "What about you?"

He sheathed his knife in his boot. "I do well enough with this baby. But I want you to keep the rifle close to you at all times."

Shelby was silent for several moments. "Do you think they'll find us?"

"Not if I can help it. And if they're stupid enough to try to take us on, they'll soon regret it," he predicted with a grim smile.

She couldn't keep her eyes off the gleaming metal. "I know I should feel comforted by that statement, but I'm afraid I don't feel all that reassured. Personally, I'd rather have a few tanks and heat-seeking missiles at our disposal."

Jed chuckled and shook his head. "Nothing like a little overkill, love."

"Not as long as it gets the job done."

Shelby began shivering when the sun went down. It had grown so dark she couldn't see past her hand. Jed had draped the blanket over her, but she still felt cold inside.

Sensing her discomfort, he moved closer and curved his arm around her. She gratefully burrowed against his body, feeling his body heat seep in as she laid her head on his shoulder.

"Things didn't turn out the way either one of us expected them to, did they?" she said softly.

"No." His reply was more an exhalation.

"You were late getting back from your trip."

He smiled at the fact that, despite everything, she was aware of his schedule. "It was one of those things."

"A problem with your mission?"

"More like a problem with one of my men."

She rubbed her cheek against his shoulder. "Is it something you can talk about?"

"Not really," he admitted, then relented. "Basically, I found out one of the men I'm responsible for has been working for both sides."

"You mean there are still double agents out there?"

He grinned. "They didn't stop with the end of the Cold War. Some people are greedy, and if the other side will pay them enough they're more than willing to forgo their principles."

"That's disgusting," she snorted. "I hope you took care of him. But I guess someone like him can't just be fired, can he?"

"I didn't have a chance to handle the situation before I had to return here, but I intend to take care of it before any more damage is done. For now, he's being watched by someone I know I can trust."

Which means Jed will be leaving soon. Perhaps not long after we return to Los Angeles, she thought to herself. *And I'll be left behind. Again.*

A cold lump settled in the pit of her stomach. She had nurtured a hope that their candid talk might have altered things between them. She should have known better. How could she hope to basically change a man's way of life?

Jed felt Shelby's withdrawal as surely as if she had physically pulled away from him. He wondered how she would feel about him if he told her why he felt the way he did. How it was so much easier not to pin all your hopes on one person because then you couldn't get hurt when that person left you.

His father had left his mother when she told him she was pregnant, because he hadn't wanted to be saddled with a family. His mother had left Jed as a baby because she didn't want to be bothered with being a mother. His grandparents hadn't known what to do with a child who grew up angry and bitter. They'd never stopped to realize his actions were a result of their own verbal bitterness toward their daughter at "dumping her problems on them." They'd turned Jed over to the state because they couldn't handle him. Even the state hadn't been able to control him. Only Smitty had understood that Jed's anger needed to be channeled into something productive. The older man had kept him so busy with anything that required physical exertion that Jed hadn't had time to ponder the negatives in his life.

Eight years with the DEA after college gave him a taste of life on the wild side, and he found he was perfect for it. Later on, Warren had heard of his skills and had recruited him to work for his department.

The last few years Jed was able to do what he did best—clean up messy situations. His dark coloring allowed him to make his way through South American cities or the Middle East without suspicion. His knack for picking up the local vernacular also helped.

He admitted that now that he was over thirty-five, the wear and tear on his body and nerves was getting to be more than a little too much, but he wasn't sure he was ready for a desk job just yet. The adrenaline rush his assignments gave him had turned him into a danger junkie. The nine-to-five routine wasn't all that appealing to him.

Except more than a few changes had occurred in his life in the past year and a half. The biggest one being Shelby, and the joy and light she'd brought into his previously bleak existence.

He looked down at the top of her head, resisting the urge to smooth his hand over the fiery strands. Jed had to admit it: Shelby gave off a warmth such as he'd never known before. He found himself tempted to curl up against her and, like a stray cat, soak up all the attention and affection she had to offer.

"Whenever I was gone, I used to think about you a lot," he said quietly, keeping her close in his arms. He'd shifted until he lay on his side with her body curved against his chest and belly. He noticed the slight tilt of her head, indicating she was interested in what he had to say. "If things started to get bad I'd remember something funny you had said or something we'd done together. There was one time I replayed that day we went to the beach over and over in my head."

"It was so cold we didn't want to take off our clothes to go swimming," she murmured. "You said you wouldn't be surprised if it snowed. So we ended up at that inn on the freeway and spent the weekend there."

Jed's lips curved at *that* memory. "That room had a nice big fireplace," he commented. "And we had plenty of firewood."

"You refused to let me wear any clothes." Her reproof didn't carry very much heat.

"You said if you couldn't wear any, neither could I," he reminded her. "At least the hotel had room service."

Her fingers pressed lightly against his arm, which rested against her abdomen. "You didn't seem to find the lack of clothing a problem."

"We turned that huge bathtub into a swimming pool."

"I wouldn't exactly say we swam in it."

Jed pushed away the lock of hair that obscured her face and dropped a gentle kiss at the corner of her eye.

"We've had some great times. We were always in tune with each other. Think about it, Shelby—we have a lot going for us," he murmured. "Are you sure you want to give all of that up because you want something that really doesn't exist?"

The moment he asked the question he knew he'd made a major error. Shelby threw off his arm and sat up. The rigid state of her spine told him he would be better off not trying to touch her again.

"Is that all you think we're about? Sex?" Her voice lashed out at him like a glass-tipped whip. The disgust in it touched a raw nerve and sent his own temper soaring.

"Not just sex. We've always had more than great sex," he growled.

"Don't break your arm patting yourself on the back, lover. I'm sure you're not the only man who's ever given a woman multiple orgasms," she drawled icily.

Jed gritted his teeth instead of giving in to his first inclination—to throttle Shelby. "No one has ever pushed me the way you have and lived to see the next day," he retorted in a clipped voice.

Shelby looked over her shoulder. One delicately arched eyebrow told him she didn't fear his less-than-subtle threat.

"Excuse me while I quake in your socks," she jeered.

Jed blinked as he tried to understand her statement. "Do you realize how ridiculous that sounded?" he said finally.

Shelby considered what she'd just said and chuckled. "It did sound more than a little crazy, didn't it?" she admitted. "But I can't exactly quake in my boots when I'm not wearing any, and the socks I'm wearing are yours." She held up one foot, still covered with his sock, as well as Meredith's shoe, which was looking decidedly worse for wear. The leather loafer might have been well made, but it was obviously not meant for mountain climbing. "Chris owes Meredith a pair of Ferragamo loafers. These were her favorites, too. She's not going to be happy they're in such horrible condition."

"I'll make sure to take it out of his hide."

"Do that. Then I want a crack at him." Shelby took vicious pleasure in visualizing Chris and Eric slowly roasting over a bed of hot coals. Her imagination took off from there.

Jed watched various expressions play over her face. He wasn't sure what she was thinking, but he had a pretty good idea she was greatly enjoying her daydream.

Later that night, Shelby found herself looking out across the mountain for any sign of light that indicated the three men were still around.

"If they're smart, they won't be having a fire tonight," Jed said quietly, accurately guessing the direction her thoughts had taken her. He wrapped his arms around her from behind and drew her back against his chest. "They're getting too close to civilization to risk being seen. Eric is too clever to take any chances now."

"He likes to frighten women." She spoke without thinking. "He likes hurting them and keeping them afraid of him."

Jed's arms tightened. "How do you know that?"

She swallowed. "From things he said to me that night. He liked the idea of telling me his likes and dislikes as he fed me pieces of meat. He wanted me to know I was completely under his power, with no chance of escape." With her back to him, he couldn't see the shadows around her eyes, but he knew they were there as she went on. "He believes a woman should know her place from the beginning. I'd told him that my father would pay handsomely for my safe return, but he didn't care about that. He doesn't even care if the woman they take can cook just as long as she keeps Eric happy." Her voice caught. "I didn't have to ask what happened if he wasn't kept happy," she said in a small voice that fairly quivered with tears. "He told me. I guess he wanted to make sure I knew what could happen if I misbehaved."

Curses the likes of which Shelby had never heard rolled past Jed's lips even as he pressed kisses along her hairline. For the next ten minutes, she listened to his idea of torture for the man, which was far more gruesome than anything she could have thought of. With each kiss came another form of torture.

"Would you really do all that?" she asked once he wound down.

"And more," he vowed.

Shelby smiled. She wondered if Jed realized he was actually making a form of commitment to her. Maybe there was hope for the man, after all.

Jed wasn't finding it easy to sleep. Not when Shelby's sweet round behind was nestled so securely against his belly. Her breathing was deep and even as she slept warm and secure in his arms.

Since he couldn't sleep, he listened for anything out of the ordinary, but all seemed quiet. He mentally mapped out the rest of their trip back. As long as they could keep themselves moving among the brush, they should be able to get down by the next afternoon.

He hadn't missed how badly she was limping now. Before they had prepared to sleep, he'd applied more antiseptic to her feet and rebandaged them. He hoped to at least keep any infection at bay.

Touching even her foot, so sore and bruised and lacerated, had him wanting to hold more of her. But her eyes had drooped with weariness and she'd looked as if she wanted nothing more than to crawl into a bed and sleep. He wanted to crawl into a bed, too. But not to sleep.

"Jed?" Shelby's soft voice drifted back to him.

"Hmm?"

"This new side of you has been enlightening."

He chuckled. "Enlightening? That's a new way of putting it."

"If you hadn't come up here after me, I probably would have died, because they wouldn't have had an easy time getting me to knuckle under to their demands," she said quietly. "One thing I've wondered, though. Why did you come up alone? Why didn't someone from the sheriff's department or a ranger come with you?''

"There wasn't anyone available," he explained. He sensed her shock at his explanation. "They had only one tracker and he was on another job. As far as the sheriff was concerned, you were already another missing person who wouldn't be found."

"He had already written me off?" She was incredulous.

"Unfortunately, yes."

"But you didn't."

"You're a stubborn and very strong lady. I knew you'd make it."

Shelby smiled at his confidence. She would have rolled over to face him, but his grip kept her from moving.

"My very own James Bond. But sexier."

He nuzzled the soft area just behind her ear. "Sexier, huh?" He noticed the way she further relaxed in his arms. "I like that idea."

A coil of heat settled deep within Shelby's stomach, and it had nothing to do with Jed's hand covering her abdomen. If she shifted her body just a little, his fingers could easily find their way beneath the waistband of her shorts.

"James Bond would take advantage of a situation like this," she prompted, then gasped when his hand shifted upward until it covered her breast. His thumb and forefinger rolled her nipple to an aching erectness. She arched her back as he cupped her breast.

"But I'm not James Bond," he murmured in her ear.

Shelby found it difficult to formulate her thoughts. "Good, because I'd rather have you, no matter how grouchy you can be."

Jed took her earlobe between his teeth. "Would you say I'm grouchy now?" His other hand slipped beneath her pajama bottoms and palmed her aching center, his fingers delving inside her moist warmth. "Hmm, I'd have to say *you're* not the least bit grouchy. It looks like you're showing me how wet you are instead." He savored the rich music of her soft throaty moans, knowing he was causing them. As he teased the tiny nub that intensified her pleasure, she arched back and his hips bumped against hers.

Shelby's head tilted, pressing against his throat even as her lower body rocked forward against his hand. "I want you!" she keened, pressing her nails into his wrist.

Jed didn't need a second invitation. He practically ripped his zipper as he tore the tab downward, at the same time pulling down her pajama bottoms with his other hand. With one strong thrust he was firmly inside her, feeling her tight walls squeeze around him. He muttered a curse, fearing he would finish before he'd even begun. But he had the sanity to rein in his enthusiasm and deliberately slowed his strokes as he cupped her from the front, pulling her against him.

Shelby twisted her head so she could see his face. "Jed," she whispered. Her lips were parted and moist, and her tongue trailed across her lower lip.

His mouth slammed down on hers even as his body filled her, his tongue thrusting inside to twine around hers in a lover's dance.

The urgency was rabid in their veins, but it was left unspoken that they wanted their lovemaking to last as long as possible. Shelby's hips slowed even as Jed's thrusts became lengthier, though still deep.

It was as if this was their only way of telling each other what they truly felt. Jed couldn't divulge his deepest secrets, but his body could let her know how much he wanted her with him always. Shelby still feared that if she pressed for more, this time Jed would be the one to leave, but with her body she could indulge her every fantasy. She could pretend he would always be hers.

Jed had always marveled how well they fit together. Even their breathing rhythms were in sync as they raced for that fiery pinnacle. As always, the explosion was intense, their eyes glowing as they looked into each other's soul.

And when they fell off that pinnacle, they didn't drop into dark depths but into an abyss of bright light that showed them what they were looking for. If they cared to hang on to it.

Chapter 9

"Once we get back to civilization I am going to make you buy me a steak," Shelby told Jed as he packed up the backpack and made sure his weapon was fitted snugly in its holster, against his back. "I'm talking about a nice big one. Along with a large order of onion rings, garlic bread and a very good bottle of wine. Maybe two."

"Anything else?" he asked, amused with her request. And not all that surprised. The idea of a meal made up primarily of red meat seemed an excellent one right about now.

"Cheesecake for dessert," she decided. "A very large piece. I have several days of barely eating to make up for."

"I'll make sure all your requests are filled," he told her as he tightened the laces of his hiking boots. He then straightened up and grasped her shirttail. Smiling that smile that sent electric charges through Shelby's blood, he pulled her toward him, indulging in a long, satisfying kiss. Shelby melted against his chest with the idea of taking more, but Jed ended it reluctantly. He knew they needed to get out of there. He pulled away, regret etched on his face.

"What do you say we go in search of that steak," he said, picking up the backpack and settling the straps on his shoulders. "Something tells me we're going to need the red meat for energy."

He reached for Shelby's hand, lacing his fingers through hers as he prepared to climb down, but she held back.

"I'm glad you were the one to come up here for me, Jed," she said softly. A small smile curved her lips.

He smiled back. "You weren't too sure of that in the beginning."

She nodded. "I know. I guess it was because I couldn't imagine your coming up here. You see, when I was praying for help, I said I wouldn't care if a trained gorilla rescued me as long as it was soon. It didn't take me long to realize you're definitely better than a gorilla."

Jed shook his head in wonderment. He knew she had to have been scared, but yet she had somehow kept her sense of humor intact. He should have known his lady would have lots of guts. He leaned over and kissed her again. Not a heated kiss like the night before, but one that promised a great deal. Later.

"Let's get down this mountain," he told her, helping her to descend the rocky slope.

For a while during their hike Shelby paid closer attention to their surroundings than she had the day before. But because Jed was in a hurry, she found herself having to take two steps to his one. It wasn't long before she found herself out of breath.

"Enough," she wheezed, pulling on his hand. "If we don't stop right now I'm going to run out of air."

"I don't think there's any way that can happen."

She huffed and puffed as she painfully tried to catch her breath. "Oh, yes, there is. And I'm living proof. I need to stop, Jed."

He frowned as he scanned the trees and scrub around them. "We can't take too long."

"All I ask is a minute to rest." She dropped down onto a boulder and reached for the canteen hanging from his belt.

Jed studied her with a sharp eye. He couldn't miss her heaving chest or red face. "I thought those aerobic classes you took every day and your personal trainer kept you fit."

"My classes and my trainer ensure my fitness for walking fast or running on fairly level surfaces. I wasn't meant to climb up and down mountains like a goat," she argued. She took several sips of water, then handed him the canteen. He tipped it up and drank. "I was meant to walk the mall at a reasonable pace or run through an airport to catch a flight."

Jed shook his head. "Good thing I'm along to help you through this new experience of yours." Feeling prickles of unease travel along his nape, he looked around. "Are you ready to go?"

Shelby couldn't miss the taut expression on his face or the tension lacing his voice. "What's wrong?"

Jed merely shook his head and grabbed her arm. "Come on." He kept his voice low as he walked more rapidly down the slope. "We've got to move."

With trees and brush around them, he hoped they could remain hidden. Jed knew their luck might not hold. The thought had even occurred to him that the men might have decided to climb all the way down to Meredith's cabin and lie in wait for them there. If so, they would have easily found his car and figured out he'd be returning in that direction.

He cursed himself for not bringing along his cell phone, even though there was no guarantee it would have worked in the heavily wooded region. He hadn't wanted the extra weight in his backpack, and he'd assumed he would have no problem rescuing Shelby. So far, he hadn't.

He told himself not to worry if he didn't have to. He had promised Warren he'd bring Shelby back safely and that was exactly what he intended to do.

As they hiked down the steep trail at an even faster pace than before, Shelby felt the tension in the air, as if an electric storm was approaching. She fully expected to see small animals fleeing and birds flying to safer territory as if danger stalked their heels. She knew she didn't dare ask for any more stops. Jed sensed something was wrong, and she wasn't about to dispute his hunches.

It wasn't all that much later that Shelby felt burning pain radiating out from the bottom of her feet, up through the back of her heel and along her leg. She glanced down and saw blood seeping through the bandages. She gritted her teeth against the pain and concentrated on not limping.

She was thankful Jed was too busy scanning their surroundings to keep a close eye on her. She knew he sensed she was right behind him and that was all that mattered.

As they reached the end of their journey, Shelby felt herself drooping with weariness. She stumbled several times and once fell to the ground.

"I'm all right," she told him, raising herself up on her hands, then scrambling to her feet. "I wasn't looking where I was going and I must have tripped over a rock."

Jed frowned when he noticed the bloody bandages. "Damn," he muttered, squatting down and examining her feet. "Those need to be changed."

"We can take care of that when we get down." She hated herself for feeling afraid, but the back of her own neck was prickling like mad. Was this what Jed felt when danger was close? "We need to go, Jed! You said so yourself."

He looked up and didn't miss the terror in her eyes. Along with that he saw the trust in her gaze. Trust in him. He was glad to see it. He didn't want her trust to be misplaced. "Yeah." He straightened up.

Shelby compelled herself to ignore the pain in her feet as she almost ran to keep up with Jed.

"If this is what you do as a spy, you're a better person than I am," she panted. "My killer instincts are better in the malls than out here."

"And you do a great job there. Just remember, we're going to get through this," he told her, still keeping to the path he felt was safest.

Shelby was so intent on keeping up with Jed that she ran into his back when he stopped abruptly. She opened her mouth to ask what was wrong, but he motioned for silence. She settled for standing on tiptoe and looking over his shoulder. Her mouth widened to a soft O when she saw the clear blue lake, looking as peaceful as it had that day that seemed so long ago. They'd reached the clearing where the Ackerman cabin was situated. She recognized Jed's black sedan parked along one side of the building.

"It's too quiet down there," Jed murmured, his gaze sweeping the scene with a sharpness guaranteed not to miss even the smallest detail. His body was tight with tension as he surveyed every inch of ground.

"Wouldn't it be quiet because no one's there?" she whispered, although she couldn't figure out why she felt the need to speak so softly.

"Quiet, yes, but not this quiet. You have to remember it can be quiet even when someone is around." He lifted his head as if sniffing the air.

She watched his action. "The way those men smell we should be able to detect them a good ten miles away," she muttered, wrinkling her nose with disgust. "I swear, a skunk that had been dead for a week would smell better than them."

Jed lifted an eyebrow. "You ever smell a dead skunk?"

She screwed up her face. "No, and I'm not too sure I'd care to."

"You wouldn't. Not unless you want your sinuses cleared for the next month." He absently touched the hard lump slung over his shoulder. The rifle resting there should have been comforting, but it wasn't. Right now, he wanted them out of there. Damn! Why did he feel as if all hell was going to break loose any second? "We've got to pray they've given up and haven't gotten down here ahead of us," he told her. "Just head straight for the car. Don't stop for anything and don't look back. I'll deactivate the locks before we reach it so all you have to do is open the door, dive in and keep your head down. Use the cell phone to call for help."

"Why do I have a bad feeling about this?" Shelby asked, wishing she could will away her sense of alarm. She wondered if spending the past few days with Jed had attuned her senses in some way.

"Don't even think about it," he muttered, double-checking his rifle.

"Let me take that." She pulled on his backpack straps. "It will be one less thing for you to worry about."

"If it proves too bulky, just drop it and keep on running. There's nothing all that important in there."

"I'll definitely leave it behind if there are any of those awful cereal bars left," she quipped, draping the straps over her shoulders.

Jed looked down at Shelby. He couldn't miss the flushed state of her cheeks, the taut expectancy in her body and the emerald sparkle in her eyes as she gazed up at him. Her face wasn't clean of anything but makeup, but he couldn't imagine she had ever looked more beautiful to him than she did just now.

Dammit, she was getting off on this! Her hair was dirty and tangled around her face, her clothing more suited for a ragbag than a boudoir. What exposed skin wasn't filthy was marred with scratches and bruises. But it was as if none of this mattered to her. For now, the danger was pumping up her adrenaline and giving her the kind of high no drug could duplicate. She was ready for battle and actually looking forward to it. She was proving to be her father's daughter, all right.

Jed couldn't stop himself from touching her. He cupped the back of her head with his free hand and pulled her toward him. The moment their lips met, his tongue thrust inside for a raw, heated kiss. Pretty soon his other hand, still holding the rifle, rested flat against her spine as she melted against him. He didn't want to worry about her! He refused to think something could happen to her. Most especially, he didn't want to think Eric and his boys had gotten down here already and had disabled the car. Damn, he didn't want to feel anything!

"Shel." He broke away, breathing hard. "I swear if you ever pull a stunt like this again, I'll keep you tied to the bed for the rest of your life."

The Shelby of the past would have been angered by his arrogant statement. The new Shelby merely smiled.

"And the same goes for you, darling." She patted his cheek. "Now, can we get out of here? I'd kill for a long hot shower."

Images of a naked Shelby in his shower danced briefly before his eyes before he pulled himself together. Jed grabbed her hand and pulled her down the last few hundred yards.

Shelby's fingers were on the passenger-side handle and Jed reaching for the driver's door when a familiar taunting voice and the mocking sound of hands clapping invaded their tenuous relief.

"Congratulations, I figured you'd end up as mountain lion bait. You're better than I thought you'd be."

Jed slowly turned. Eric, with his nephews on either side, stood a little way off, at the edge of the clearing. While Eric's high-powered rifle was cradled in his arms, those of the two younger men were aimed directly at them. Out of the corner of his eye, Jed could see Shelby slowly dropping the backpack and standing stiffly. He thought of every curse he could remember. Considering the state of her feet, he doubted she would be able to run if he ordered her to. Certainly not fast enough to outrun the two nephews.

Now that he saw Eric up close he could detect the faint signs of madness in his eyes. There would be no talking to this man. He would rather fight to the death, and Jed sensed that he usually won. But this time things would be different. Jed was going to make sure Eric didn't walk away with Shelby. The bastard would have to lose his life.

As Jed stood there, hands at his sides, his mind rapidly worked out scenarios and rejected most of them. After all, their opponents had their weapons in the open, ready to shoot.

"Drop the gun," Eric ordered abruptly. His eyes were cold and flat. The lack of emotion in his gaze was chilling.

Shelby had remained silent until then. "What are we going to do?" she murmured, just loudly enough for Jed to hear.

"I'm not giving up my weapon," he said in a voice meant for Eric.

Shelby winced. "That isn't what I wanted to hear."

Eric smiled. There was no humor in his action, just pure animal glee. "You stole my woman. I don't like hippies stealing my women."

Jed raised his head, staring straight at him. If it was to be a battle of wills, so be it. "She was mine first. And I hate to tell you this, but the hippie movement pretty much died out in the seventies." Out of the corner of his eye he could see Shelby bite down on her lip to keep her mouth shut. Good. It looked as if she had learned when to remain quiet. Keeping watch over her sensibilities wasn't part of the plan right now. He had to keep his attention centered on the man standing before him.

"Then you shoulda kept a better eye on her," Eric advised, still smiling. "Because she's mine now."

"I don't think so. I intend to keep a very close eye on her."

Eric still cradled his rifle in his arms like a baby. "You know I can't let you just walk out of here."

"It might be a better idea if you did," Jed replied conversationally, as if they weren't talking about anything more important than the weather. "Ordinarily, I'd just kill you and be done with it. Hell, I'd probably receive a medal for doing so. After all, you've been kidnapping women and killing them when you're tired of them. The law looks down on that kind of behavior. You would have been better off if you'd remained up that mountain with those boys and not ticked off people down here."

"Who you calling a boy?" Chris scowled, stepping forward.

Jed stared at him long and hard. "I see you have a broken tooth. I promised someone to give you extra hell from her."

Chris looked wary. "You mean that other bitch is alive?"

Jed nodded slowly. "Not only alive, but she's hungry for your blood. I promised her I'd take care of you."

Chris growled a curse and stepped forward with the intention of taking Jed on himself.

Eric's upraised hand stopped him. "He's trying to rile you, and it sounds as if he's doing a good job of it," he murmured, still keeping his eyes on Jed. This was an opponent he could respect. A man who understood the value of a good fight. Eric only had to study Jed's stance and the equally flat look in his dark eyes to know he was a skilled fighter. The question was, who was better? His gaze flicked downward to Jed's boots. "You carry a knife?"

"Doesn't everyone?"

Shelby shifted from one foot to the other. "What the hell is going on here?" she demanded. She couldn't miss the escalating tension in the air.

Jed didn't take his eyes off the three men as he reached down and pulled out his knife. "Just a friendly discussion, love." He placed the rifle on the top of the car. "We have a few things to settle."

Her eyes widened as she realized his intent. "To settle," she whispered fiercely. "You're going to kill each other!"

He kept his eyes on Eric. "No, I'll put him out of commission and will only kill him if necessary."

"This is between us," Eric told his nephews, as he laid his rifle down and pulled out a large, jagged-edge hunting knife. He held it easily, as if it was a part of his body. "You just make sure it's kept fair."

"Are you going to make sure you fight fair?" Jed taunted.

Eric's features darkened. "I always fight fair."

Jed's lifted eyebrow told another story. Shelby was relieved to see he appeared to feel just as comfortable with his blade.

Eric looked in her direction. "You tell him you're coming with me and I'll let him live."

She gave an unladylike snort. "Do you really expect me to believe that? No thanks. I'd rather see Jed kill you."

"Then, sweetheart, you better be prepared to mourn your man."

Shelby had never thought of herself as a blood-thirsty person. She wasn't fond of horror movies, couldn't read horror novels, and the sight of her own blood—or anyone else's, in fact—made her feel queasy. Yet she stood there and watched the two men drop to a crouch and circle each other. Not once did they take their eyes off each other as they gauged who would attack first.

She noticed that Chris was watching her with hungry avarice. She felt like a small animal under the dark gaze of a feral predator itching to tear her apart. She didn't doubt that if the two older men killed each other, Chris would take his pleasure with her. She thought of Jed's rifle still lying on the car roof. She vowed to herself that Chris wouldn't have a chance to do anything. She forced herself not to even glance at the car so Chris couldn't figure out the direction of her thoughts.

She held her breath as the two men circled the area with easy steps, each waiting for that first opening.

Obviously tired of the cat-and-mouse games, Eric went first. He lunged forward, swiping the blade sideways. Jed leapt back and barely missed having his chest sliced open. Shelby bit down on her lower lip to swallow her scream of fear. She refused to give in to hysterics. No matter the cost, she had to be brave for Jed's sake. The last thing he needed was to be distracted by her.

"Your boyfriend ain't gonna last," Chris told her. "My uncle learned to use his knife in the war and no one ever survived."

"There's always a first time."

Chris stared at her. "The first thing we're going to do when we get you up to our place is get you out of those clothes. You won't need them up there."

She refused to show any reaction to his words. She had no doubt Jed would do everything possible to keep her safe. "The first thing I'm going to do is make sure you're thoroughly deloused before seeing you're thrown in a cell where you won't see the light of day for the next fifty years," she answered.

Andy looked uncertain as he watched the two men. Eric now sported a gash on one arm and another cut on his cheek.

"What if she's right?" he muttered.

"Shut up!" Chris ordered, scowling at his brother. "Have you ever known Uncle Eric to lose before? Just shut up and make sure that bastard doesn't cheat." His eyes narrowed as he studied Jed's agile moves. Jed evaded Eric's attacks and deftly parried every slash of the blade.

Shelby couldn't stop her gasp of horror when Eric's knife flashed silver in the sun, then lifted to reveal red on the edge. Blood dripped down Jed's arm.

"Very good," he exclaimed. If he felt pain he showed no sign of it. He feinted left, then went right and lashed out at Eric's face.

Eric grinned. He didn't seem to notice the blood trickling down his own cheek. "I'm the best." He showed no signs of exertion.

"Not anymore." Jed's eyes gleamed a pure silvery gray. "You can't win this time, Eric. I wouldn't be surprised if you do a little extracurricular sniffing when things get boring. Or do you just wander into town and shoot out the streetlights? Nothing like keeping your nephews at the emotional age of six, is there? That way they might not learn just what a freak you are. What do you tell them about your nightmares? Not the truth, I bet."

The other man's face grew mottled with fury. "*No!*" he screamed as he rushed at Jed.

That was all he needed. Jed spun around with one leg outstretched and easily kicked Eric's knife from his hand, while adroitly twisting his own knife and burying it in Eric's chest.

Eric's mouth opened and closed like that of a fish out of water. His eyes bulged as he stared at Jed. Eric first dropped to his knees, then fell forward on his face, his body motionless.

There was no expression on Jed's face as he stepped back. "There's no joy in this kind of win," he said quietly.

"Uncle Eric!" Andy ran forward and dropped to his knees by his uncle's body. He turned him over and stared at his lifeless face. "He's dead! Chris, he's dead!" he told his brother. "What're we gonna do?"

"You bastard, you killed him!" Chris lifted his rifle at the same instant Shelby and Jed realized his intent. There was no place for Jed to hide and he was too far away from his rifle. But Jed could make sure the bullet wouldn't prove fatal. As the rifle spat out a bullet, he dived to one side. A faint *oomph* left his lips as the bullet buried itself in his chest. He cursed himself for not diving fast enough.

"*Jed!*" Shelby screamed. She didn't stop to think. As Chris turned in her direction, she reached for the rifle. She lifted the stock and didn't bother to aim, but just pressed the trigger. Bullets spat out, trailing fire, and easily connected with her target.

Chris looked more surprised than anything as splotches of red blossomed across his chest.

"I should have taken the other bitch," he said as he fell down.

Andy looked from one to the other, then at Shelby, who kept the rifle trained on him. "Don't make me use it again," she warned.

He slowly raised his hands.

Shelby kept her eyes on him as she hurried to Jed and checked his wound.

"I've had worse," he told her between clenched teeth as she tore a strip off her pajama top and made a compression bandage. "Make him take off his pants, boots and socks." He started to chuckle at her look of dismay, then groaned as he realized laughter wasn't a good idea. "Believe me, sweetheart, he won't run if he doesn't have any clothes."

Shelby did as he instructed. Andy was in too much shock to argue as he pulled off his clothing, and Shelby used his belt to tie him to the porch post. She ran back to Jed and gasped when she saw the blood-soaked bandage.

"Just use the cell phone to call for help," he ordered in a voice racked with pain.

She gently cradled his face, gray and deeply etched with pain. "You can't die on me." Her voice was broken and husky with tears. "I swear, Jed Hawkins, if you die on me I will never forgive you."

"I don't intend to die just yet, sweetheart. Not when I have to make sure you don't get caught up in anything this crazy again," he told her just before he passed out.

Chapter 10

Shelby hated hospitals. She also hated waiting. It didn't take her long to decide waiting in hospitals was more torture than having a root canal.

Once Andy was secured to the porch post, she had followed Jed's orders and used his cell phone to call the sheriff's office. When she gave her name, they'd reacted immediately, and a deputy was quickly on the scene with an ambulance close behind. The young deputy took one look at her disheveled figure and Jed's bleeding, unconscious form cradled in her arms and gestured for the ambulance to stop near them. He glanced at the other three, read Andy his rights and took him into custody. Shelby fought to ride in the ambulance with Jed. She vowed she wasn't going to leave him alone. The technicians took one look at the hysterical lights in her eyes and didn't argue.

They wasted no time transporting Jed to the hospital, and he was immediately wheeled into surgery. Shelby fought the personnel wanting to tend her own wounds until she was assured she would be given any word of Jed's condition right away. Her thoughts were so focused on him that she didn't stop to think about Meredith being in this same hospital.

By now, Shelby had had antiseptic applied to her scratches and the blisters on her feet tended to and carefully bandaged. She was allowed to shower and was given a pair of surgical scrubs to wear. For someone who had been looking forward to a long hot shower, she had probably taken the shortest one in history.

"Miss Carlisle." The deputy who had arrived in summons to her call held out a paper cup of coffee. "All I can say is it looks like mud and tastes like mud, but you won't find a better drink to give you that much-needed kick start."

She smiled her thanks as she accepted the cup. She sipped the hot brew and grimaced at the bitter taste. "To be honest, it tastes more like battery acid, but I have an idea I'm going to need this to get through the next few hours." She dropped into a plastic chair, rubbing her eyes with her fingertips.

"I talked to Mr. Hawkins when he first showed up in town. I'm glad to see he was successful in finding you," the deputy told her. He apparently was used to the battery acid that doubled as coffee, since he didn't blink as he drank deeply. "Have you had a chance to talk to your father?"

She shook her head. "Right now, I'm more worried about Jed. My father will understand that I want to wait until he's out of surgery, because Dad's going to want to know about his condition." She looked at the man's nameplate, where Rick Howard was inscribed. "How's your prisoner?"

His mouth twisted. "Sitting in his cell sniveling like a baby. He said he only did what his uncle and brother told him to do. None of it was his idea."

Shelby had no sympathy for Andy. "I admit he begged his brother not to hurt me when the man tried to get rough, but I think if Chris had pressed the issue Andy would have just backed off." She felt queasy as she remembered the sight of blood pouring out of Chris's chest. He had died within seconds of being shot. Her aim had proven to be erratic but deadly. She quickly tamped down the feeling of guilt with the reminder that the man deserved what he'd got. "I shot to stop him, not kill him."

"Miss Carlisle, you did what you had to do. The man would have killed you without batting an eyelash. You saved Mr. Hawkins's life," Rick said simply.

Her smile wobbled dangerously as tears threatened to fall. She had been battling the weeping willies since Jed had been taken into surgery. She knew it had to do with the shock of being free, of seeing Jed shot and later overhearing the doctors and nurses jabber back and forth about a punctured lung, low blood pressure and rumors of more internal injuries. It was as if they'd done all they could, yet didn't have a lot of hope of his making it.

When Shelby had used the shower, she'd stood in the tiled stall and given in to the urge to cry until she thought there were no more tears left. Obviously, she'd been wrong—she once again felt the sting in her eyes. She sniffled, then blinked when she saw a swatch of white in front of her face.

"Easier than wiping your nose on your sleeve," Rick told her with a faint smile.

She smiled her thanks and accepted his offering. She blew her nose and wiped it.

"He actually fought that man with a knife," she said with wonder in her voice. "A man who had lived like an animal for years. It was obvious he didn't have a conscience." She shuddered as the realization of what would have happened to her if Jed hadn't shown up finally hit her like a nuclear bomb. He had fought to keep her safe and was badly injured as a result.

"Oh, my God." She clapped her hands over her mouth to stop the sobs. She had no idea she was shaking violently even as Rick put his arms around her.

"Hey," he soothed, patting her back awkwardly. "Everything's going to be fine."

"No." She shook her head. "Jed's in critical condition. They said so. He could die because of me. And I never got to tell him—never got to tell him . . ." Her teeth chattered so violently she couldn't finish.

Rick realized she was in shock. "We need a doctor here!" he shouted.

Shelby didn't protest when a doctor quickly checked her over and noted her widely dilated eyes. A hypodermic was swiftly administered.

"Miss Carlisle." Sheriff Rainey strode toward her, looking self-important. "I'm sure you realize we need a statement from you. I'm glad to see Mr. Hawkins was able to rescue you. Usually we don't like having a civilian around, but I guess this was one time it worked out.'' He rambled on, oblivious to her traumatized condition.

"Sheriff." Rick's voice held a warning. "Mr. Hawkins was taken to surgery and Miss Carlisle's just been given a tranquilizer. Maybe this should wait until later, when she feels more up to it.''

The older man scowled. "I'll say when things are done here, boy. You just remember who's in charge.''

Shelby's drug-induced fog cleared just enough for her to see another uniformed man standing in front of her. His words came through as if a filter had been placed between them.

"Who are you?'' Her words were slightly slurred.

He puffed up his chest. "I'm Sheriff Rainey. I admit I told Hawkins I didn't think he'd have a chance in hell of finding you, but I'm sure glad to see I was wrong. Just wish our tracker had been here to get on the job right away, but you know how it is when your resources are small. Sure hope those boys didn't hurt you none. Violate you or anything.'' He peered at her sharply. "Anything you need to tell me? We have good doctors here who can help you.''

Shelby slowly stood up, her world shifting under her feet as she fought to keep her balance. She felt as if she was standing at the end of a tunnel and the sheriff was at the other end.

"You weren't going to send anyone in to try to rescue me,'' she said, fuzzily trying to make sense of what the man had said. He would just let them take her and not do anything about it? "You were going to let those animals have me.''

He shifted uneasily. "Well, ma'am, as I said, our tracker wasn't available, and we don't have a large force here. I'm just glad Hawkins was able to get you out of there."

"Wasn't available," she repeated. "You son of a bitch." Her mumbled words sounded more like *thon of a bith*, but that didn't stop her from letting fly with her fist. Considering her shaky balance, it was a miracle her clenched fingers made a solid connection with the man's nose.

Sheriff Rainey howled in outrage and pain. He cupped his hands over his face and blood streamed from between his fingers. "You broke my nose!" he shrieked.

Rick muttered a curse under his breath. At the same time, he was working hard at hiding a grin. "Next time watch your thumb. You're lucky you didn't break it," he advised Shelby under his breath.

"Damn! That really hurts!" She shook her injured fist. The pain in her hand completely dissolved all numbing effects of the tranquilizer.

"There was no reason for that!" Sheriff Rainey shouted at Shelby. He started to advance on her.

Rick knew it was time for him to step in. "Sheriff, please remember the woman is in severe shock. She had no idea what she was doing," he said swiftly.

"Yes, I did," Shelby whispered, but luckily only Rick heard her and kept that piece of information to himself.

Rick kept talking as Sheriff Rainey was led back to an examination room by a nurse. It wasn't until the older man was out of sight that he gave in to the laughter he'd been holding in. Soon he was laughing so hard he bent over, bracing his hands on his knees. Shelby couldn't help it; she had to join in. By the time she finished, she was wiping her eyes.

She looked around the empty waiting room. "At least there was no one here to think we'd really lost it," she told him.

He nodded. "Yeah, they probably would have hauled us off to a nice padded room and not let us out for a long time."

Shelby looked down the corridor, then she collapsed in a chair with her legs sprawled out. Ordinarily, she would have been horrified by her less-than-ladylike posture. "I really needed that."

"The sheriff might not agree."

She chuckled softly. "Do everyone a favor and take over his job." She stared down the hallway again. "I just wish I knew what was going on."

"I'm sure someone will come out soon and let you know," he assured her.

Shelby jumped up and starting pacing for lack of anything better to do. Soon too tired to pace anymore, she dropped back into the chair. Her rear had barely grazed the plastic seat when a doctor in sweat-stained surgical scrubs walked out.

"Miss Carlisle." He managed a weary smile. "Mr. Hawkins has lost a lot of blood and he had a punctured lung, but I have no doubt that with plenty of rest he'll come through just fine. He hung in there from the beginning. He's a fighter."

Shelby started to sniffle again. "Oh, damn, I'm turning into a watering pot."

"Delayed shock," the doctor told Rick, who merely nodded. "Miss Carlisle, how you've managed to stay upright this long is an absolute miracle. I checked your friend's room and there's an empty bed next to hers. I suggest you climb into it and have a good long sleep. You need it.''

"Meredith?" Guilt instantly set in. "I forgot all about her." She paused. "What about Jed?"

He shook his head. "He's in ICU right now under a nurse's watchful eye. You need to get some rest. I'll prescribe something for you to help you sleep."

"That might not be a good idea. She was just given something by a doctor, after which she punched out the sheriff and broke his nose," Rick muttered. He nodded when the surgeon stared at him as if he couldn't believe what he'd heard.

"It just goes to show there's justice, after all." The doctor chuckled as he walked off. "Room 207, Miss Carlisle. Tina, the charge nurse up there, will be waiting to tuck you in."

She shook her head. "I need to see Jed first."

The doctor started to refuse until he saw the look of stark determination on her face. He knew if he didn't agree she would probably take the hospital apart looking for him. The man heaved a deep sigh. "Five minutes and no more. He's so snowed under he won't even know you're there."

"Yes, he will," she whispered.

Shelby wasn't prepared to see Jed lying under a sheet that was as white as his features. A thick bandage covered his chest and wrapped around his shoulder. She wanted to cry at the sight of him lying there utterly helpless. Various tubes helped him breathe, while an IV bag hung near him, dripping drugs into his system as he lay unconscious. She stood by his bed and touched his hand. The fingers under her touch were unresponsive as she lifted them to her lips.

"I love you," she whispered against skin that felt warm and dry.

She wished she had the strength to argue with the nurse about staying longer, but the way Shelby's body was moving slower and slower told her she barely had enough energy to make it to Meredith's room.

By the time she staggered into the room a friendly nurse escorted her to, she felt as if she had been awake for weeks. She took one look at Meredith, asleep in the other bed, smiled fondly, then dropped onto the mattress. Curling up into a tight ball, she instantly fell into a deep sleep.

"I'll have you know I've had much livelier room-mates in my time. But I have to say I'm very glad to see you."

Shelby rolled over and opened her eyes. The white room was unfamiliar and she could feel aches and pains in every part of her body. She stared at the next bed, where Meredith was sitting up.

"You look awfully good for someone I thought was dead," she croaked, struggling to sit up herself.

"And you look terrible for someone who always looked so good first thing in the morning. I was once convinced you slept with your makeup on," Meredith countered. She fairly bubbled with excitement at seeing her friend again. "I heard you shot one of them while Jed took out the other. When did this bloodthirsty trait of yours emerge?"

Shelby nodded, then shrugged her shoulders. "It wasn't exactly the highlight of my life." She winced as another bruise made itself known when she shifted her body. "What time is it?"

"A little after two in the afternoon. You missed breakfast and lunch." When she saw Shelby's look of shock, she hastily added, "They said you needed the rest, Shel. You were on the point of collapse. The doctor still can't figure out how you functioned after the heavy-duty tranquilizer he gave you. I heard it wasn't long after you were given the happy juice that you broke the sheriff's nose. You are on a roll, aren't you?"

"*That* was the highlight of the day." She struggled to her feet, only to have the world spin around her. She abruptly sat back down before she fell down. "I need to see Jed."

"He's still unconscious. I asked about him, since I knew that would be the first thing you'd want to know," Meredith told her. "The nurse said not to worry. It's more a healing sleep." She leaned over on her side. "What happened out there?"

Shelby's mind seemed to run in fast motion from the time Jed released her bonds to their making wild love in the cave to their escape down the mountain and Jed's fight with Eric.

"More than you'd ever imagine," she said wearily. Here she'd just woken up and she already felt tired. And hungry. She looked around. "You didn't happen to keep anything from lunch, did you?"

Meredith shook her head. "I'm sure one of the nurses can find you something." She pressed her call button.

Shelby climbed off the bed and walked over to her friend. "I am so glad you're all right." Her voice shook with suppressed tears as she hugged her tightly. "When I saw you lying on the floor and all the blood around you, I thought for sure you were dead."

"I probably would have been if a deputy hadn't come by when he had," Meredith admitted. "When I heard they'd taken you, I was so afraid." Her eyes were dark with concern. "Then I heard all those stories about those men, rumors they were kidnapping women but nothing could be proved. I wasn't sure if I worried more about you stuck up there with them or your having to survive without running water," she joked feebly.

"Considering how horrible they smelled, there was no doubt they had no idea what water was," Shelby quipped in turn, wrinkling her nose. "By the time Jed got me back down, I think I smelled almost as bad as they did."

Meredith lay back against her pillows. "Amazing, isn't it? Here you talked about wanting Jed to turn into this super Alpha man and it sounds as if he did just that. It's enough to make a woman's toes tingle."

What came to Shelby's mind was the night they'd made love in the cave. She'd left scratches on his back as she practically ravished him. They had mated like two young animals, and she couldn't remember ever feeling as satisfied as she had that night.

"When I said I wanted to see another side to him, I had no idea just what I would see," she murmured.

Meredith's eyes widened. "Really? What exactly are we talking about here?"

Shelby gave the smile of a supremely satisfied woman. "Let's just say when he reveals his other side, he reveals it in spades."

"Damn!" Her friend snapped her fingers. "And to think you offered him to me and I said no. When will I learn?" She affected mock disappointment, then continued her interrogation. "Did you tell him you love him?"

"Not so he could hear me." Shelby inspected her nails. All were broken and sported chipped polish. It was going to take awhile to bring them back up to snuff.

"So you decided to keep him after all. Now what?"

She shook her head. "I have no idea. All I know is I don't want to give Jed up. And he acted as if he wasn't about to give me up. But he isn't going to give up his work, either."

"Are you willing to settle for a long-term affair?" Meredith asked gently.

"I could give you excellent examples of unmarried couples who have been happy together for years and married couples who have barely lasted a year," Shelby replied evasively.

"Yes, but you still want to take the chance, don't you?" Meredith pressed.

She nodded. "I guess I'm more traditional than I thought I was, but I don't want to give Jed up, either. I'd like a chance to figure out this new side of him first." She knew she couldn't tell her friend Jed's true occupation or the secrets her father had kept all these years.

Their conversation was interrupted when a nurse walked in. She looked decidedly perky that afternoon with her ash blond hair pulled up in a bouncy ponytail tied with a bright pink bow. A stethoscope hung around her neck against her floral-print top.

"Well, well, I see our newest resident is awake." She walked over to Shelby and picked up her wrist, pressing her fingertips against her pulse point as she studied the second hand on her watch. "How do you feel?"

"As if I went ten rounds with King Kong," she groaned. "I can't imagine why anyone would want to mountain climb. It's too hard on the body."

"I'd say you did just fine." She unrolled the blood-pressure cuff and wrapped it around Shelby's arm. "Let's just make sure all the signs are normal, shall we?"

"I'm breathing. Isn't that enough to tell you I'm fine?"

The nurse smiled as if Shelby was a precocious child who had said something amusing. "I'll be the judge of that." She noted the blood-pressure readings, jotted them down on a chart and looked up. "Then we'll see what the doctor says when he gets in, hmm? You've become a special patient to us. We want to make sure you're well taken care of."

Shelby glared at Meredith, who hooted with laughter.

"If you could see your face!" Meredith squealed, flopping back against her pillows.

"It's a good thing you're in a hospital," she muttered between clenched teeth. "That way you can receive medical care without having to wait."

By the time the doctor arrived, Shelby was practically foaming at the mouth. She had asked for a report on Jed and was told he was doing fine. Which meant nothing to her. She wanted to see him for herself.

"Bridie's in charge of ICU this shift, and believe me, you don't want to go up against her," the nurse Shelby now knew was named Faye warned her. "No one in their right mind wants her for an enemy."

Shelby gave in, but she wasn't graceful about it. She had tried to call her father on his private line, but only received a recording to leave a message on his voice mail. She decided against leaving one and made a mental note to try again later.

As soon as the doctor declared she was fine, Shelby took advantage of the small bag of her clothes Rick was kind enough to bring in and quickly showered and dressed. She stared at herself in the mirror and grimaced at the bruises mottling her face and chest. She discovered makeup couldn't effectively cover them up.

"Now you look as if you were only in a minor battle instead of an all-out war," Meredith told her.

Shelby sat on the edge of her bed. "I guess when we talked about having an adventure, we didn't expect such a painful one," she said. She inwardly winced at the bandage covering part of Meredith's forehead. Her friend's very expensive haircut had been altered when the doctor had to shave a section of her scalp to stitch up the cut she'd sustained when her head hit the dresser. But Meredith wasn't too worried. The doctor, attractive, single and very interested in Meredith, was taking her out to dinner as soon as she was released from the hospital. Meredith had informed Shelby of that fact soon after he'd left.

"Only you would be robbed, attacked and badly injured and end up dating the doctor," Shelby teased as she brushed her hair.

"I wanted this experience to have a positive effect on my psyche," Meredith replied with a regal air as she watched her friend leave the room. "Give tall, dark and handsome a kiss for me, will you?"

Shelby dimpled. "No problem there."

Her smile wobbled as she approached ICU. From what she'd heard of Bridie, she expected to find an Amazon manning the desk. Instead, she found a petite brunette fireball who seemed to handle ten crises at once without batting an eyelash. Dressed in a pink top and pants, she looked too delicate for the demands of nursing, but Shelby soon realized the woman was more than capable of taking on anything thrown at her.

"Mr. Hawkins has been resting comfortably," she reported after Shelby identified herself. "In order for him to recover, he needs all the rest he can get. Which means the last thing he needs is a visitor guaranteed to raise his blood pressure."

Shelby looked down at her tan-colored walking shorts, long-sleeved ivory blouse and navy-and-tan print vest. Navy leather flats completed her outfit. While she had been able to brush her hair into a semblance of order and add makeup, she still didn't feel she looked her best.

"Believe me, he's safe. I'm afraid I left my see-through negligee at home," she said flippantly. She instantly regretted her words.

"Laughter is fine and good, but Mr. Hawkins lost a great deal of blood before he was taken into surgery. He also has a punctured lung that had to be repaired," the nurse informed Shelby with a forbidding expression on her face. "Which means he needs quiet and rest."

"All I want to do is go in there, make sure he's all right and sit there and hold his hand," she argued. "I just want him to know I'm there for him."

Bridie studied her for a long moment. "Did you really break the sheriff's nose?"

"Yes, I did, and I'd do it again."

A smile softened Bridie's features. "Go on in, but make sure to stay out of our way when we need to be in there. And be sure to let me know if he wakes up."

Shelby almost ran into the room. She pulled a chair close to Jed's bed and picked up the hand that was free of IV tubes.

"Haven't you slept enough?" she asked softly. "Honestly, Jed, you're the least-lazy person I know. There were mornings you'd be up at the crack of dawn so you could jog a few miles while I was still sleeping like the dead." She grimaced. "Bad choice of words. You know what I mean." She gently stroked the back of his hand with her fingertips. "I'd honestly feel much better if you would open your eyes for me." She leaned over so she could whisper in his ear. She smiled as she whispered just about every provocative suggestion she could think of.

"Are you sure some of those are physically possible?" a voice, raspy from the heavy drugs filtering through his blood, whispered back.

Shelby blinked rapidly to keep her tears in check. "I have no doubt you'd find a way," she murmured, pressing the back of his hand against her cheek.

Jed fingered the tears streaming down her cheek. He opened his eyes, but the usually clear storm gray was hazy.

"Did they tell you they thought I was going to die?" he rasped.

She shook her head, lying. "You lost a lot of blood and had a punctured lung." That much, at least, was the truth.

"Don't worry, I've had worse." He licked his lips. "How about some water?"

She started to reach for the cup, then reared back. "I better call the nurse in first. She might not want you to have any right away."

Jed frowned. "No nurse poking and prodding me just yet," he argued.

"Trust me, it's safer for me to call Bridie first than for her to come in and find out you woke up and I didn't call her," she told him as she reached for the call button.

"A regular tyrant, huh?" He made a face. "I've met more than my share of those."

"Something tells me you haven't met anyone like her before," Shelby said sagely.

Barely a minute later, Shelby knew she was right. From the moment Bridie swept into the room, she took charge. Shelby was pushed out of the room while the doctor was called and Bridie busily checked Jed's vital signs.

Shelby paced the corridor with barely leashed impatience until the doctor left the room.

"He's already doing better than I expected," he told her. "But he won't be getting out of here as soon as he'd like."

She smiled. "Such as today?"

"He thinks he can get up and walk out of here. Little does he know he couldn't even stand up without falling on his face," he replied. "Hopefully you can keep him down."

"Not exactly down, but I can make sure he doesn't do anything stupid," she assured him.

"I have to admit the two of you have given this town a lot to talk about," he muttered as he went on his way.

Shelby immediately returned to Jed's side. She wanted to laugh at the look of disgust on his face. There was no drug-filled haze in his eyes now.

"I wanted out of here," he grumbled. "And the doctor said I wouldn't make it past the door."

Shelby picked up the gown lying on the foot of the bed.

"There is no way in hell I'm wearing that thing," he stated. "Not when it leaves my butt hanging out."

"But it's such a gorgeous butt," she murmured, leaning over and dropping a kiss on his lips.

Jed started to reach up to deepen the kiss, then groaned as the stitches protested his movements.

"Sorry, hot stuff," Shelby cooed, amused by this new side of his nature. Her tiger was effectively leashed. "It looks as if you're going to have to behave yourself for a while."

"We'll see about that."

Judging by the set expression on his face, Shelby wouldn't have been surprised if he made sure he was fully healed by the end of the day.

Chapter 11

"I don't understand it. Every time I've called my father on his private line I only get his voice mail," Shelby complained to Jed later. He'd slept on and off during the day, and she alternated between his bedside and Meredith's. "I'm really worried about him. I didn't want to phone him until you were out of surgery, and since then I've made about five calls and I haven't heard from him." Her eyes were shadowed with worry. "And I don't want to just leave a message."

Jed looked away. "I'm sure he's all right."

"Yes, but once he heard I was back and all right, you know he'd want to get right up here. Unless..." She turned sharply and stared at him. The old Shelby wouldn't have noticed his evasive manner. The new one couldn't miss it. "What aren't you telling me, Jed?"

He looked her square in the eye. "Nothing."

Shelby resisted the urge to lean over and pull his hair hard to get his attention. "My lie detector just went off with bells ringing. What's wrong with my father?" Dread filled her heart as worst-case scenarios filled her mind. "He's not . . . ?"

"No, he's not dead," he said hastily, easily reading the meaning behind her fear. "But he did suffer a minor heart attack and had to be hospitalized."

"Minor. . . ?" She jumped to her feet. "There's no such thing as a minor heart attack! Why?" The answer came to her as soon as she asked the question. "It was because of my abduction, wasn't it? He couldn't handle the shock and collapsed." For a moment she felt as if she couldn't catch her breath. "I knew his heart wasn't strong," she cried, castigating herself.

"Hey, it's not your fault," he reminded her. "Warren was upset about you, yes, but he was also furious because he wasn't getting any answers from the law up here. I think he would have come up right away, but I arrived just after he heard about you. Instead, he met me at my plane and collapsed just as I reached him. As soon as he was able to talk to me at the hospital, he gave me the information. I drove up here immediately."

Shelby felt torn. Jed was here, but her father was down in L.A. Both men needed her, but deep down, she knew her father needed her more. She got up, walked over to the phone and dialed for an outside line. In no time, she had left a message for her father's doctor with his answering service, insisting he call her immediately. She dropped back into her chair to wait for the phone to ring.

Jed watched her with the intensity he was known for.

He started to ask himself what it would be like to have someone care and watch over him like that, then quickly backpedaled. He'd already heard from the nurse how Shelby had refused to rest until he was out of surgery and how she had fought to see him afterward because she wanted to make sure for herself he was all right. And she had come here as soon as the doctor checked her over. So far today, she had left the room only when the nurse had shooed her out.

He could see her bruises were starting to fade but were still faintly visible under a careful application of makeup. He commented on them.

She wrinkled her nose. "I feel as if I look like a patchwork quilt. All purple, blue, black, green and yellow."

"What happened after I got shot?"

"What happened?" She looked confused, then laughed uncertainly. "Jed, you were there."

He shook his head, then wished he hadn't; he was positive rocks were rolling around in it. "A lot of times you lose bits and pieces of your memory when a trauma like that happens to your body."

Shelby hesitated. She looked as if the memory she retained was painful.

"You were able to move in and kill Eric before he killed you," she said slowly. "Chris went crazy seeing he was dead and he shot you. You obviously realized what he was going to do and threw yourself to one side. The trouble was, you didn't do it fast enough. He still shot you in the chest." Pain crossed her features. "I guess it was my turn to go crazy after that. I don't even remember reaching for the rifle. I kept shooting, and when I finished Chris was dead and Andy was scared he would be next. You were barely conscious but you told me to take Andy's belt and use it to secure him to the porch railing. After that, I used your cell phone to call for help. By the time a deputy and ambulance arrived, you were unconscious and bleeding badly."

She paused for a moment to collect her thoughts and compose herself. "You were very lucky. The doctor said you were obviously a fighter and not willing to give up easily." Her fingers trembled as they stroked the back of his hand. She stared across his chest at his other hand, anchored down with two IVs, one delivering painkilling drugs and the other giving him much-needed fluid. "I gather it was assumed you wouldn't make it," she whispered, fighting tears that threatened to erupt. "Damn!" She pulled a tissue out of the box on his bed table and blew her nose.

"Hey." Jed curled his fingers around her hand. "You know what happens when you cry. Your eyes turn all red and swollen and your nose turns even redder. Are you sure you want that nasty color to add to that patchwork skin of yours?" he teased gently.

She laughed through her sniffles. "You charmer, you." She stared at the bulky bandage covering most of his chest and suddenly, the enormity of his injuries and her father's medical condition hit her like a ton of bricks. For someone who hated crying, she found herself unable to stop. She laid her head on the edge of the bed and sobbed uncontrollably. Deep within her, she was stunned she could still cry. For someone who only cried at weddings and movies, she was making up for lost time.

Jed cursed under his breath at his lack of mobility as he reached out to cup the back of her head with his hand. When he realized none of his soothing was working, he started to panic. Instead of searching for the nurse's call button, he settled for bellowing.

"Excuse me, but you don't happen to be the only patient we have here." Bridie swept in like a hurricane. She took one look at Shelby and was at her side in a second. She covered Shelby's shoulders with her small hands and lifted her up.

"Do something!" Jed ordered, anxiety making his voice harsh.

"She's still going through delayed shock," she said crisply, as she gently forced Shelby to sit back in the chair. "Considering everything she's gone through the past few days it's a miracle she hasn't broken down completely. She must have been running on sheer willpower to do as well as she has done. All right, honey, everything's all right," she crooned as if speaking to a small child.

"I killed a man!" she wailed.

Bridie looked at Jed over Shelby's head. "I think I should call one of our counselors to talk with her. Help her calm down. The last thing she needs is any more tranquilizers. They only mask the symptoms instead of helping them."

He nodded. "Her father suffered a heart attack right after she was kidnapped. I think she's trying to take on a load of guilt."

"No wonder." Bridie pulled out another tissue and handed it to Shelby, taking the soggy one out of her hand and tossing it in the wastebasket. "I'll make the call now. You just keep on talking to her. I'll be back in a minute."

Jed's estimation of the tough-natured nurse rose several notches as Bridie left the room.

"Shelby, you did what had to be done," he said urgently, wishing he could take her pain from her and make it his own. He was only too used to the nightmares a situation like this could cause. But Shelby had been lucky enough to have been raised in an atmosphere of love and laughter. Not darkness and danger. "If you hadn't killed Chris, he would have finished me off, then taken you, and you would never have been seen again. That animal would have dragged you back up that damn mountain and used you in ways I don't even want to think about. I almost wonder if he wouldn't have killed his uncle if Eric had killed me instead of my killing him. Living up there so long turned those men into mindless creatures who only thought about their own desires. I just had to look at Chris to know he wanted you—and would have done anything to keep you. If you stop to think about it, you know what I'm saying is true."

Shelby raised her head. Her eyes were huge, shimmering emeralds in her pale face.

"I understand what you're saying," she whispered. "He wanted to kill you because he felt you took me from him, and he wanted his possession back. I think he was starting to see his uncle in the same light. They had been up there so long they lived by their own rules.''

"There was more to it than that," Jed told her. "Chris was one of those who was just pure mean through and through. It wouldn't have mattered where he lived, Shelby. He still would have ended up dead sooner or later. Someone like him isn't meant to live long.''

"Except I might not have been the one to kill him," she said, so softly he had to strain his ears to hear.

Jed patted the edge of the bed and Shelby didn't hesitate in accepting his unspoken invitation. She settled carefully beside him and rested her cheek against the section of his chest that wasn't injured. Pretty soon, the comforting warmth of his body was enough to soothe her. They were still curled up together when Bridie returned.

"Ms. Carlisle?" The nurse appeared in the doorway. "Dr. Ryan will be in her office until six. She suggested you stop by to see her." She frowned at Jed, who pasted an extremely innocent expression on his face.

"You suggested I do what I could," he said in self-defense.

"That wasn't exactly what I meant," she said dryly. "Just make sure she sees the doctor, all right? She can help Ms. Carlisle cope with the pain and guilt she's experiencing right now." She pointedly closed the door after her.

Jed wanted to tell her that he himself would help Shelby. After all, who better to understand what she was going through than someone who had lived most of his life in shadowy parts of the world?

"I'm so tired," Shelby mumbled, draping one arm across his waist. She closed her eyes and within moments fell asleep.

Jed's arms tightened around her. He ignored the pain making itself known as his medication wore off. All he cared about was Shelby. He focused on ignoring the discomfort and soon fell into a light doze.

Even while asleep, Jed's senses had no problem picking up another presence. His eyes snapped open and rested on a woman seated in the chair Shelby had vacated. If she hadn't been wearing a hospital name badge he wouldn't have been sure why she was there. He guessed she was a few years older than he was, and keen of mind, if her sharp gaze was anything to go by. In other circumstances, he'd think she was a cop.

"You the shrink?"

"That's what my diploma says." She smiled, her brown eyes twinkling. "So this is the lady who broke Sheriff Rainey's nose."

"Broke his nose?" he repeated. He wondered what else Shelby had kept from him.

She nodded. "I'm Liz Ryan. It seems Ms. Carlisle is using sleep as an escape." She kept her voice low so as not to disturb Shelby.

Jed looked down at the feminine form in his arms. "Sometimes that's the best thing to do. Unless she starts dreaming."

"I spent a little time talking to Andy Larson," she explained. "He was a bundle of nerves and the sheriff was afraid he might injure himself. I'd say his uncle and brother had him completely under their power."

He rolled his eyes. "Please, don't bring up that low-self-esteem garbage everyone uses as an excuse nowadays, okay? I watched those three out there for quite a while before I was able to snatch Shelby back. Maybe he didn't have his hands all over her the way the others did, but he knew what was going on and he allowed it to happen. If he'd had his chance back there he would have shot me. He's acting like the scared little boy for sympathy, because he's afraid of going away to prison for the rest of his life. The courts will view him as an accomplice in the kidnapping of at least five women and murder of at least four. I'd say he has a lot to worry about, wouldn't you?"

Liz didn't blink during Jed's quietly spoken statement.

"Since I'm not an attorney, I guess I don't need to worry about replying to that, do I?" Her gaze flicked over Shelby, who still hadn't stirred. "It's amazing that a civilian like you could just march up that mountain, find Ms. Carlisle and bring her back down again with little fuss."

"There wasn't a fuss until we ran into the three mountaineers," he said wryly. "They sort of ruined our idea of a nice leisurely stroll down the mountain. So tell me, how are you related to a cop?"

Liz smiled at his astute grasp of her questions. "Rick said you have government identification, but you're not like any Fed he's ever seen before."

"And he's seen a lot in his long career?" he drawled, with no malice intended.

She shook her head.

"Then maybe it's because I'm not a Fed," he suggested.

Liz waited patiently for Jed to say more, but he just as patiently remained silent.

"I've had experience in helping patients cope with delayed stress," she said finally as she rose from the chair. "I think Ms. Carlisle will need someone to talk to about the shock of the past few days."

"Someone such as you?"

She inclined her head. "Women tend to relate easier to women. Talk more freely. Bridie can get ahold of me when Ms. Carlisle's ready to talk." She smiled as she looked down on Shelby's slumbering figure. "Until then, just give her lots of love and TLC, and for all we know, she may come through with few scars." She headed for the door.

"Tell me something," Jed called out quietly. "How come someone with your savvy is up here in the sticks instead of in the big city raking in the money?"

Liz stopped with her hand pressed against the door panel. "Maybe because the demons can't find you as easily up here," she replied, before walking out.

Jed shifted his position a bit to ease the discomfort in his shoulder.

"You can't stop flirting with women, can you, Hawkins?"

He looked down. "How long have you been awake?"

Shelby opened one eye. "Long enough to hear you flirt with the pretty doctor."

"I wasn't flirting," he groused.

She carefully sat up so as to not jar his body and ran her finger along his dark brow. "Then why are you frowning? Feeling guilty, are we?"

He batted her hand away as if it was a pesky fly. "Because you're saying ridiculous things."

"I'm a woman. It's allowed." Shelby ran her fingers through her hair, fluffing the matted strands. She lifted her arms over her head and stretched. "And here I thought I'd slept enough."

Jed watched her hungrily. He figured either the painkillers had completely worn off or his pain had decided to travel in a southern direction. He adjusted the covers in hopes of covering up his "condition." It was too late. Shelby's eyes followed his movements.

"My, my, isn't modern medicine wonderful? I'd say you're getting better by the moment," she drawled, carefully edging off the bed so she wouldn't jostle him too badly.

Jed gritted his teeth against the discomfort in his lower region. At that moment, he would gladly have given his soul for just a few minutes of private time with Shelby. Any pain he would suffer as a consequence would be gladly endured.

As if reading his thoughts, she smiled.

"Bridie would probably kick me out of the hospital and make sure I never got back in," she said softly, trailing her fingertips across the back of his hand.

He swore under his breath. "Don't even think I'd let her get away with it."

"Are you kidding? That woman runs this place like a drill sergeant." She'd started to walk to the door when the phone rang. Jed inclined his head, silently asking her to answer it.

"Mr. Hawkins's room," she said crisply, then relaxed when she heard a familiar voice. "Daniel, how are you? And most especially, how is my father? I just heard about it. Yes, I'm fine other than some cuts and bruises. I was very lucky.'' She slanted a telling glance at Jed. ''I was kept overnight in the hospital for observation, but Jed, the man Daddy sent up here, was shot by one of the kidnappers.'' She was silent for a moment. ''No, nothing serious, but he'll be here for a while.''

''Not if I can help it,'' Jed muttered darkly.

Shelby waggled her fingers to ask him to be quiet. ''The tests showed no serious damage then?'' She gave Jed a thumbs-up. ''Yes, please tell him the good news and that I'll be there as soon as possible.'' She grimaced. ''All right, you don't want him excited. I understand that.''

''I wouldn't mind getting a little excited,'' Jed muttered. ''A lot excited would be even better.''

She glared at him and returned to her conversation. ''But you say his tests are good and he's doing better?'' Her shoulders slumped. ''All right, you can tell him. I'll stay on here for another day or so, then I'll be back.''

She hung up, looking more frustrated than ever. ''Why can't I be with my father?'' she demanded. ''The doctor said Daddy's better, but he needs to be kept quiet, with no added stress. And while seeing me would be positive, he's afraid he'll get overexcited, so he wants to break the news to him quietly and monitor him first.'' She shook her head. ''It doesn't make any sense. I thought you told me he only had a minor attack.''

''That was his condition when I left him,'' he explained. Any thoughts of finding a way to tumble her into his bed had disappeared. "The doctor is telling you Warren's fine, but yet he's not fine. Which is it?"

"His health is very precarious," she said slowly. "The doctor is recommending that he retire as soon as possible. He will not be able to continue with his work."

Jed was silent for so long, Shelby began to wonder if he had actually heard her.

"It won't be the same without Warren at the helm," he said quietly.

"If he retires, what happens?"

He looked momentarily confused by her question. "Someone would be appointed to take his place."

"How? Who?"

He shook his head. That was an answer he wasn't going to give her.

She wandered over to the window and adjusted the blinds so she could look out. The view of the mountains was majestic, but for the moment, Shelby couldn't find any joy in the postcard picture before her.

"Would you be considered for the position?" she asked abruptly.

"Maybe, but there are others who have been around longer than me who would be under consideration," he replied without thinking.

She didn't turn to face him. "But could you apply for it if you wanted to?"

Jed had never considered himself slow, but he was surprised he hadn't caught on to her train of thought faster.

"I could, but I won't."

Shelby's shoulders stiffened when she heard his reply. She kept her back to him. "Why am I not surprised?" she murmured, more to herself than to him.

Jed stared at her back. What was he going to say to her now? Where was his glib tongue, which had never failed him before?

Never failed you before? a little voice in his brain jeered. *What about that night in your apartment when she stormed out of there like a hurricane after telling you she never wanted to see you again? If those scum hadn't kidnapped her, she would have made sure you couldn't get hold of her. She'd even gone so far as to come up here to make sure she wasn't around when you got back. So, idiot, what are you going to do about it?*

Shelby turned around. "I should have realized you couldn't change overnight," she said in a low voice. "After all, the angry kid found his niche—why would he want to give up all that excitement he has every time he goes out on an assignment? A desk job wouldn't give you that danger high, would it? I can understand better now, Jed. It's a part of you. And you obviously feel it's a necessary part and there's no room for anything or anyone else in your life." Her fingers were clasped tightly in front of her. "I'm going to check on Meredith. She'll be discharged, although now that she's met a very eligible doctor I'm sure she won't be all that eager to leave." She started toward him, then checked her movement. "I'll talk to you later."

In Jed's mind, her statement wasn't all that hopeful. Not when he didn't have a chance in hell of going after her if she decided to leave the hospital.

As if to remind him that things were even worse for him this time around, the low, throbbing pain in his chest rapidly built up to major agony. He seriously thought about calling the nurse and asking if it wasn't time for another lovely, mind-numbing painkiller.

Damn. He was getting too old to get shot.

Chapter 12

"Now let me get this straight. You dumped Jed.
Jed flew off on one of his business trips. You came up
here with me. The cabin was broken into by two Ne-
anderthals with more brawn than brains. I was injured and you were kidnapped. Jed came back, your
father had a heart attack and Jed came up here to
rescue you."

Meredith ticked each item off on her fingertips as
she sat cross-legged on top of the bed. "He rescued
you. I'm sure the two of you had a lovely reunion in
some little hideaway." She determinedly ignored her
friend's blush. "Then our mountain boys found you
again or you found them. Jed fought for you, killed
the guy, his nephew shot Jed and you shot the
nephew. We're all here at the hospital when you find
out your father needs to step down because of his
health, so you thought Jed would conveniently take

over and skip all that lovely international travel and stay home with you. Except you found out he didn't have that in mind, so you've dumped him again. I swear, you two are better than a soap opera."

Meredith rolled her eyes under Shelby's glare. "I am your best friend, Shelby. Have been for so many years I can't remember ever not knowing you. But I will not wallow in self-pity with you. You knew from the beginning what Jed was like. You once told me he was always honest with you. Did you think he would suddenly change?"

Shelby threw her pillow at Meredith, who easily caught it with both hands. "I hate it when you're logical. And yes, I hoped he would change. There's nothing wrong with that."

Meredith hugged Shelby's pillow against her chest. "Shel, when I regained consciousness, the doctor told me that if the deputy hadn't been so prompt in answering the alarm I would have died. They didn't even tell me what happened to you right away because they weren't sure how I would handle it. As soon as I started feeling human again, I got to thinking about it. You came up here in an attempt to get away from Jed, and instead, you were thrown back with him. I came up here because I didn't know what else to do with myself. I still don't know exactly what I plan to do with myself, but I'm going to do my damnedest to find out."

Shelby was stunned as she listened to the formerly frivolous, party-hearty Meredith speak so seriously. "Is this along the lines of you 'seeing the light'?" she asked.

Meredith tipped her head back and studied the ceiling. "I think it's more like I'm realizing I don't want to grow old alone." She smiled uncertainly. "I couldn't be any worse a mother than my own mother was, could I?"

Shelby shook her head. "I don't think I'm hearing correctly. You're thinking of becoming a mother?"

Meredith leaned forward confidentially. "And why not? Have you gotten a really good look at Dr. Taylor?"

Shelby had seen the man and was surprised her friend was interested in someone who wasn't drop-dead gorgeous, didn't hold a high-powered position or have his own stock portfolio. But Shelby had noticed the way he looked at Meredith, as if she was a dream come true. Meredith had dated more than her share of losers, and Shelby wanted to see her good friend with someone who realized just how special she was.

"I've seen him, yes," she said hesitantly.

Meredith straightened up. "He wants to teach me to fish."

Shelby couldn't believe what she was hearing. "Fish? *You?*"

She nodded. "He said it'll only work if I'm willing to bait my own hook."

"With worms?"

"They're supposed to be the best," she loftily informed her.

Shelby hopped off the bed. "Now I know I've heard everything. The world is going insane. I don't know if it's the water or the clean air up here or what, but I do know I'm getting out of here before it affects me, too."

"You told me that when those men had you, you promised yourself if you could see Jed again, you wouldn't press for a commitment. You wouldn't even say anything to him about his having to take these trips," Meredith reminded her. "You realized what was important was being with him and taking advantage of the time you had together."

Shelby took a deep breath. "I really hate you."

Meredith smiled. "No, you don't. You just hate it when I'm right."

Shelby rested her palms flat against the closet door and began bumping her forehead against the smooth surface.

"Now if I did that, I'd probably shake something important loose," Meredith observed. "Doesn't that hurt?"

"I'm hoping the pain will wake me up out of this crazy dream," she said between clenched teeth. "Unfortunately, it doesn't seem to be working."

"Maybe you need to do it a little harder," Meredith said, straight-faced.

Shelby spent the rest of the afternoon on the telephone, talking to Warren Carlisle's doctor and nurse and getting hold of her father's housekeeper, who broke down and cried when she heard her voice. It took Shelby several moments to assure the older woman she was all right. She had checked her business answering machine and jotted down messages, but had no desire to return them just yet.

She didn't bother calling Warren's office. She was certain Jed had already taken care of that; besides, her father had many capable employees. She wondered if they were agents, also. She had already noticed that the drowsy look of a man under painkilling drugs had quickly disappeared the longer Jed was awake. By now, she decided on a sour note, he was probably jogging around the hospital parking lot without even breaking into a sweat. She looked up from her note taking when Faye walked in with medication for Meredith, who was still suffering from horrible headaches.

"I guess I should get out of here, since you probably need the bed space," she commented.

"We would have kicked you out if we needed the bed. That's the nice thing about our actually being more a medical center, in a sense, than a hospital. Our serious cases are airlifted out, and it's quiet right now," Faye explained. "Just don't expect room service." She handed the small paper cup to Meredith and waited for her to swallow her pills. "I have to admit you three have sure livened this place up. We haven't had this much juicy gossip since the time two skiers tried to make love on the ski lift late at night and practically froze to each other."

Meredith made a face. "Sounds painful."

Faye giggled. "It was to them."

"And here we thought small towns had no excitement," Shelby said.

"Oh, we do, but we keep it to ourselves. We don't want it ruined with too many city folk coming up here," the nurse teased. "Mr. Hawkins is back from his tests if you want to go up and see him."

Shelby went on instant alert. "What tests?"

"He was experiencing a lot of pain, so they wanted to make sure there weren't any other problems cropping up," she explained. "The doctor figures because there's old scar tissue so close to this present wound, it's creating problems in the healing process."

Shelby could feel Meredith's gaze on her. "He'll be fine. He's tough," she murmured, refusing to look at her friend.

"And probably waiting for someone to come in and kiss his boo-boo better."

Faye looked from Meredith to Shelby and back again. "I thought there was something going on . . ." She brightened up. "If there's not—?"

Meredith waved her hand back and forth. "Don't even bother. She gives him away and he refuses to understand he's supposed to go with someone new. I had him for all of two seconds and enjoyed every bit of that minuscule time. Even if he didn't know it." She heaved a deep sigh and made a great show of inspecting her nails.

"I'll look in on Jed in a little while," Shelby said, eager to end this conversation as quickly as possible.

"According to Bridie, a Do Not Disturb sign would be in order where you two are concerned." Faye quickly left before Shelby had a chance to respond. Or retaliate.

"I really like this place," Meredith commented. "Everyone is so . . . real."

"You're only saying that because of the good doctor. Once the lust wears off, you'll decide this is a one-horse town and you'll be rarin' to get back to all the fun we have," Shelby replied, feeling more than a little put out at her friend's keen observations.

When Meredith didn't respond, Shelby cast her a quick glance. Instead of anger, she saw something that looked suspiciously like pity.

"I think I'll check on Jed," she muttered, making her escape.

"Good idea. I'm sure he'll be glad to see you."

Unable to leave without having the last word, Shelby waited until she was walking out the door to say, "At least I didn't have to wear braces all through high school."

She should have realized Meredith wouldn't let that go.

"Better braces than major zits my junior year. Right before the prom, wasn't it?"

Shelby smiled to herself. She should have known better than to get in a contest with Meredith. Her friend's mind was a virtual database of information.

Shelby didn't head for Jed's room immediately. She stopped in the unoccupied visitors' waiting room and gazed out the window. The mountains looked as if she could reach out and touch them. She shuddered as she remembered her unplanned trek up one of them. She placed her palm against the glass, feeling the coolness against her skin. With the sun setting, the sky was brilliant orange, turning the peaks a dark navy blue and deep purple.

"So beautiful and so dangerous," she murmured.

"Like you."

She didn't turn around for a moment, but remained standing at the window. When she did turn, she found Jed seated in a wheelchair. A hospital-issue robe was pulled around him. She wanted to smile at the sight of him in the hospital gown held together with only a couple of ties in the back, but thought better of it.

He remained in the doorway, as if blocking it. Even now there was a sense of power around him, as if all his senses were on alert to make sure an enemy didn't lurk nearby. It wasn't just his job that made him this way; it was an integral part of the man himself.

"Making your escape?" she asked lightly, deliberately ignoring his provocative comment.

He grimaced. "Bridie could put the fear into anyone."

"Even you?"

He grinned slightly. "Even me. The woman is a tyrant worthy of Kublai Khan."

"I heard that, Hawkins!" Bridie's voice could be heard from down the hallway. "Just for that I'll use ice water for tomorrow's sponge bath."

"See what I mean? The woman's middle name is Sadistic," he confided.

"Maybe she just knows you better than you'd like to think," Shelby replied. "I heard you had a great deal of pain. Something about old scar tissue acting up."

"Perils of old wounds in the vicinity of new ones." He verbally brushed it off.

"The one when you were mugged by that kid in Cairo?" she asked archly.

He still watched her with that unnerving stare of his. "Not exactly."

"The enemy?"

He slowly nodded.

She learned more about him now each time they were together. How had he managed to keep his life so neatly divided into two separate parts? Who was the man she had once known as Jed Hawkins? It was mind-boggling.

"Were any of those scars from your childhood or muggers?" she asked, trying to keep her questions light and airy instead of demanding. It wasn't easy. She found herself growing cold inside every time she thought of the Jed she first knew and the man she had come to know the past few days.

How had she missed the little signs all these months? His way of making sure he sat against a wall facing the restaurant doors. The way he always seemed to know if someone got too close to them. The invisible protective cloak he seemed to throw around her wherever they went. The times he seemed to be on alert for something only he could sense. She suddenly felt sick to her stomach. Had her attraction to him blinded her that much?

"Childhood scars were more internal," he said with a closed expression.

"I need to go to my father," she said finally, for lack of anything else to say. "I want to make sure for myself that he's all right, so I thought I would leave in the morning."

His expression didn't change and his eyes remained focused on her face. "I'll drive you."

She gaped at that statement. "You aren't ready to leave here."

"I know what my body can handle," he countered. "And I'll be doing the driving."

"The doctor won't allow you to leave so soon," she argued.

His lips twitched in a mirthless smile. "That's why hospitals have something called Against Medical Advice. I've signed myself out of hospitals more times than I can count."

"You've done your job, Jed. You brought me down safely, so it's best if you stay here and let the staff take care of you while you recuperate. My father would tell you the same thing."

"We'll take my car." With that, he turned the wheelchair with an ease that spoke of familiarity with the device and rolled down the hallway.

Shelby could have followed him to his room and told him there was no way she was going to allow him to drive her back. She could have reminded him that her father would order him to stay in bed until he was fully healed. She could have insisted she didn't need protection any longer. But she had no doubt that no matter what she said to him, how long or vehemently she argued, he would still be in that car with her the next day. Not only in it, but driving.

"One day, he has to learn he can't have it all his way," she murmured, walking out of the waiting room. "And one way or another, I'm going to show him that's the way the world works. He's going to find out he can't win all the arguments. Or do things the way he wants to. One day I will win."

"I do believe of the three of us, I'm actually in the best physical shape. Perhaps I should be doing the driving."

"*No!*"

Meredith didn't show the least bit of petulance at Shelby and Jed's simultaneously shouted retort.

"It was a thought." She stretched her legs along the back seat and picked up the paperback book she'd been reading for the last half hour.

Shelby envied her friend's ability to lose herself in a book while riding in a car. All Shelby ever ended up with was a queasy stomach.

She hadn't been surprised when Jed signed himself out of the hospital that morning, but was furious when he insisted on driving, after making arrangements for her car to be picked up by an agent and driven back to L.A. She may have lost the battle but refused to lose the war. She knew her plan was successful when she saw the look of resignation on his face as a chirpy-looking Meredith appeared by the car as Jed was loading their luggage. It had taken Shelby two hours of pleading, cajoling and outright bribery to convince her friend she needed to return home that very day and no, the good doctor would probably not forget Meredith within twenty-four hours. Shelby gave up her favorite copper silk blouse for the cause, but she considered it a worthy expenditure—she'd give anything to avoid all those hours alone in the car with Jed.

She cast a sideways glance toward the passenger seat. Jed's lips were tightly compressed. His set expression and the white lines around his mouth told her he was in pain, but he wasn't about to admit it.

"Anyone want to stop?" she asked.

"No." Jed looked straight ahead.

Shelby glanced in the rearview mirror. "Meredith?"

Her friend looked up with feigned wonder on her face. "Am I supposed to say yes or no?"

"Say no and you won't have to walk the rest of the way," Jed kindly advised.

Meredith held up her book. "I'm fine, thank you very much, but stopping at a drive-through for something to drink wouldn't be amiss, would it? And maybe a cheeseburger?"

"We'll do that," Shelby said, as if she had made the final decision.

Driving Jed's car was far different from driving her sportier model. His was a much larger and heavier vehicle but had unbelievable power. She kept one eye on the speedometer to keep to the legal limit. The last thing she needed was to be stopped for speeding. Although she was certain Jed had the resources to ensure that a ticket would be erased from the Highway Patrol computer.

For now, he sat silent in the passenger seat. She had to admit she was surprised he hadn't fought her too much on the driving issue, but one look at his newly sharpened features told it all. He had signed himself out when he wasn't ready. And he was paying the price. She vowed that once they reached the hospital, she was going to have him hog-tied and thrown into the bed next to her father's, where he would have no choice but to stay there and recuperate.

"You do realize you owe me big-time for coming along," Meredith told Shelby when they finally stopped for lunch.

Jed had excused himself for a few minutes and walked away. Even though he was slightly gray in the face and was dressed more casually than usual in a dark red, crew-necked sweater and jeans, he turned more than one woman's head.

"You already conned me out of my copper blouse," Shelby reminded her. She stared across the room at the menu board and wondered if she had time to get a chocolate shake. Right now she needed all the comfort she could get.

Meredith finished the last of her drink and set down the cup. "I know I was discharged today with my doctor's blessing, not like someone else who's so stubborn he checked out long before he should have." She ignored Shelby's warning glare. "I was getting to know the man of my dreams, and instead, I'm chaperoning the two of you. Guess where I'd rather be?" She went on without waiting for a reply. "Which I believe means I deserve the earrings that go so beautifully with that blouse. After all, they are a set and shouldn't be separated, should they?"

Shelby leaned across the table. "You are pushing the limit."

Meredith merely smiled. "You were the one who was so eager to go up there, so don't try to put any blame on me."

"She only went because she didn't want to see me again. Too bad her plan didn't work."

They looked up to find Jed standing by their table. Shelby noticed he held a paper plate in his hand, which he placed in front of her.

Shelby's mouth watered. A slice of cheesecake.

She turned to face him when he sat down. "Thank you."

While there was no smile on his lips, there was one in his eyes. "Thought this might calm you down some. As for our traveling buddy..." He handed Meredith a tall cup.

Her eyes lit up. "A chocolate shake. You are forgiven," she said regally, taking the plastic spoon he handed her and promptly digging into her treat.

"Thank you so much," he said sardonically.

Shelby cast him a sly glance. "Are you regretting returning with us?"

"Not at all. I'm learning more every moment I'm with the two of you," he replied.

She felt a frisson of unease travel up her spine at the expression on his face. "Such as?"

Jed stirred his coffee in a leisurely manner even though he hadn't added anything to it.

"I've found out that there's a lot more to you than I ever knew about. I fully intend to ferret out that hidden part of you until there's nothing about you I don't know."

Shelby was grateful she hadn't had her shake in her hand. Otherwise, it would have surely dropped from nerveless fingers.

Chapter 13

"I must say, being with you two is better than sitting home watching a television sitcom," Meredith announced when Shelby dropped her off at her condo. Shelby had walked her up to her front door. Meredith looked past her, smiled and wiggled her fingers at a stone-faced Jed, who merely inclined his head in acknowledgment. "Goodbye, Jed," she called out. "It's been entertaining."

Smiling brightly, she turned to face a glaring Shelby. "He's so cute when he's serious, isn't he?"

"What has happened to you?" Shelby demanded.

"You should know, since you suffer from the same ailment. It's called love." Meredith patted Shelby's cheek. "Give your father a hug from me. Then do yourself a favor." She lowered her voice. "Make an effort to show Jed what a great thing he has in you. You just might get a very nice surprise." She unlocked her door, quickly disarmed her security system, and stepped inside. "Call me later and let me know how things go," she ordered.

"I hope your good Dr. Taylor snores like a freight train," Shelby said loudly just before walking off.

"He would never do that." Meredith's light response followed her down the walkway.

Shelby was still muttering under her breath when she jerked open the driver's door and dropped onto the seat. She turned to Jed and held up one hand in warning. "Not one word," she insisted in a dark voice. "If you value your life you won't say one word."

"Fine by me." He turned back to stare out the windshield. "Why don't you just drop me off at my place? Feel free to use the car to go visit your father. I can understand you're anxious to see him."

"Whatever." There was no way she was going to let him know she had another plan in mind. She turned on the radio and found some classical music in hopes it would lull him to sleep. Her goal would be easier to accomplish if he wasn't awake.

Jed settled back in the seat and closed his eyes. He was more tired than he'd realized, and he could feel painful twinges starting at the edge of his wound and moving in with relentless daggers. He slowed his breathing, willing the blood to flow slower, to allow him to drift into a dream state as the soft music soothed his tired brain.

Ordinarily, he wouldn't have tried this technique when he was with someone else. The last thing he wanted was to allow anyone to see him in a weakened state—especially Shelby. But it was a long drive to his apartment and he wanted to conserve his strength as best he could. Once he made it back there, he figured it shouldn't be any problem to get up to his apartment, where he could shed his clothing, drop into bed and sleep for a week. Once Warren knew of his injury, he would understand Jed's not coming to see him right away. The idea had barely formed in his brain before he began to fall into a light doze.

If Shelby only realized just what it meant for him to sleep while she drove. He thought it best not to let her know how much he trusted her. She was getting too out of hand as it was.

Jed wasn't sure what told him something was wrong. Perhaps the sounds of traffic were a little too loud for his neighborhood. And why could he hear so many sirens? Was there an accident or a fire nearby? He frowned as he forced himself to swim upward through the foggy gray layers of sleep.

When he opened his eyes, they were parked in a garage, with a sign nearby posting hospital visiting hours. He blinked several times and carefully turned his head. Shelby was curled up in the seat with her back resting against the door. She watched him with an unwavering gaze.

"I thought I told you to drop me off at my apartment," he said slowly. He was right; she was getting out of hand.

"You need medical attention that you'll get a lot easier here than at home," she said, so reasonably it was almost frightening. Why couldn't she be as intimidated by him as everyone else was? "So I called Dad's doctor on our way here and he arranged to have someone check you over when we arrived. You were sleeping so peacefully I didn't want to wake you."

Jed sincerely wished he could lose his temper. Except that would take too much energy, and right now he didn't have any to spare.

"I had more than enough medical attention at the hospital to last a lifetime. I'm fine," he growled, forgetting the burning pain in his chest. Damn! All he wanted was a bed! Why, for once, couldn't she do what he wanted her to?

"Are you fine?" Shelby asked softly, nodding toward his chest.

Something in her eyes told him there was more to her argument than her trying to be stubborn about this. He looked down and swore. He didn't have to touch the dark splotch on his sweater to know it wasn't water.

"You started bleeding just before we dropped Meredith off," she said quietly. "I'd already planned to bring you here to make sure it was safe for you to check out of the hospital so soon. But once I saw you were bleeding through your bandages, I knew it had to be done no matter how much you didn't like it."

"Look..." Jed bit back his instinctive argument when he looked at her fully. There was true fear in Shelby's eyes and her lips trembled. "Oh, hell," he groaned, turning to open his door. He muttered a pithy curse when a sharp pain hit his chest. Luckily, he was able to mask it before she could see him.

Shelby hopped out of the car, ran around to the passenger side and waited as Jed levered himself out. She sensed he wouldn't appreciate any assistance on her part, so she stood back, waiting for him to climb out. As soon as he closed the door, she set the car alarm and took his arm.

"I do not need any help," he said between clenched teeth as they headed for the elevator.

"I know you don't," she said airily, pulling him closer. "But take advantage of snuggling up to me while you can."

"Where did this bossy woman come from?" he asked no one in particular.

"I've always been this way. I just kept this side of my nature from you." Shelby punched the elevator call button. "Of course, being such an open and honest person, you wouldn't understand such a thing."

He couldn't help but grin when she made payback so enjoyable. "Touché."

Shelby ushered him into the elevator car. "Yes, well, wait until you hear what I'm going to tell the doctor about you."

Just before the door closed, someone joined them inside the car, so Jed wasn't given a chance to demand just what she had meant by that statement. He settled for a meaningful glare, but it didn't seem to have the power it used to. She merely gave him a serene smile in return.

Jed hated hospitals. He'd never been in one he liked. To him, they always meant being given food that wasn't fit for a dog, being awakened at odd times just to make sure he was all right, being poked and prodded and asked where it hurt when they damn well knew where it hurt. Not to mention being woken up to be given a damn sleeping pill!

He was positive this hospital wasn't any different. The doctor greeted him warmly, then turned into the consummate professional when he saw the blood staining Jed's sweater. He turned to Shelby.

"If you'll just wait outside, Miss Carlisle, while I conduct the examination," he said, glancing toward the door.

She perched on a small stool. "I'm staying."

Jed winced as he tried to extricate himself from his sweater. "Dammit, Shelby," he muttered.

She didn't blink an eye at his grizzly-bear attitude. "I want to make sure you tell the doctor everything." She smiled at the doctor. "He tends to bend the truth to his own means."

"Next time I bend something . . ." Jed said under his breath, leaving the rest of the threat unspoken. He swallowed a curse as the sweater caught on his bandage, pulling on his wound.

Shelby gasped when she saw the blood staining the white strips across Jed's chest. After his next warning look, she remained quiet as the doctor and nurse removed the bandages and examined his injury. She kept her lips compressed tightly as she saw the stitches used to close the ragged wound. The skin was badly bruised, black and purple; there was no doubt there would be a scar marring the muscled skin she remembered caressing with such delight.

The few other scars on his chest were much smaller and fainter. She knew the new one wouldn't affect her feelings toward him. But the realization of what he did for a living and what could happen to him hit her harder now than before. While he might be used to dealing with this kind of danger, she wasn't used to seeing its effects. She didn't like it.

"You're a very lucky man," she heard the doctor tell Jed. "A fraction of an inch to the left and you wouldn't be here now."

"I figured that," he replied.

Shelby blinked rapidly, but it didn't help. The edges of her world still flickered and turned a soft pastel color before turning black. She had no idea when she slid off the stool onto the floor in a graceful heap. Nor did she hear Jed shout her name in a panicked tone. If the doctor hadn't been holding on to him tightly, he would have caused further damage to his wound by trying to catch her.

"Miss Carlisle. Miss Carlisle."

Something pungent was passed under Shelby's nostrils. She batted at the offending smell and jerked her head from side to side.

"And I thought those creeps smelled bad," she muttered, opening her eyes. She was stunned to find herself lying on the examination table while a worried-looking Jed hovered over her. The nurse standing next to him, holding something in her hand, smiled and stepped back. "It's natural to faint," she assured Shelby.

"Not for me." She started to sit up, but Jed pushed her back down.

"And you figured I was the one who needed medical attention," he rumbled.

Shelby frowned at the bandages on his chest. They were white. "Where's the blood?"

"While you napped, the doctor cleaned me up and said if I don't do anything stupid, he can't force me to check in here," he told her with a smug smile.

She curled her lip. "Then he doesn't know you very well, does he?" She glanced at the doctor. "In case you haven't figured it out yet, Doctor, Mr. Hawkins doesn't take directions very well. It would be easier to just tie him to the bed."

The man looked pained. "Miss Carlisle, he's an adult. I'm afraid I can only do so much. If he doesn't want to check in, I can't force him," he explained.

She uttered a long-suffering sigh. "Then I guess it's up to me." She pushed herself off the table. It took a moment for her to keep her balance without fearing she would fall on her face. She walked over to Jed and gently placed her hands on his thighs. She could feel the play of hard muscles under her palms. She looked into eyes the color of storm clouds at dusk.

"Jed, you can't be a hero all the time," she said softly, keeping her eyes locked on his. "If you had stayed in the hospital instead of checking yourself out too early, you wouldn't have torn those stitches and started the wound bleeding again. You can't afford to take any more chances with yourself. If I had driven you to your apartment the way you wanted me to, you might have collapsed on your bed and bled to death out of pure stubbornness. Now, either you check yourself in here until the doctor says you're ready to be discharged, or I will go up to my father and tell him you are not physically ready for work. I don't think you want me to do that."

Jed uttered a soft curse. "All right," he conceded grudgingly. "But don't expect me to be pleasant about this."

There was relief in her smile. "I'll make sure you don't regret it."

He hooked an arm around her neck and brought her face closer to his. "That's a promise I'll want you to keep," he murmured, before bringing his mouth down on hers.

Shelby's head spun, as it always did when Jed kissed her. All sense of time disappeared as she gave herself up to the heady taste and leaned further into his embrace.

If the doctor hadn't coughed just then, anything could have happened. She could feel her face burning with embarrassment as she drew back. She offered him an apologetic smile. "Sometimes I have to use unorthodox methods to get him to behave," she explained.

"I'd say it worked very well," he muttered. "I'll arrange a room for Mr. Hawkins. A nurse and orderly will be in shortly," he thought to warn them before walking out.

Jed was grinning when Shelby turned back to him. "You enjoyed that, didn't you?"

She shrugged her shoulders. "I wasn't sure it would work, but I could hope. Besides, whether you want to admit it or not, you must be in a lot of pain. The ride back wasn't all that smooth."

"Not with Meredith and her lively chatter incessantly flowing from the back seat," he said wryly. "That woman can outtalk a magpie."

"Mr. Hawkins?" A nurse and an orderly standing behind a wheelchair appeared in the doorway. "Shall we take you up?"

For a moment Jed looked uncertain, but the expression was banished from his eyes as quickly as it had appeared.

"Would you mind if I tagged along?" Shelby asked. "That way, later on, I won't have to peek in every room to find you."

"If you want to."

Shelby hid her smile as she watched Jed sink into the wheelchair and allow himself to be wheeled out of the room. How like Jed to refuse to admit he needed someone. Perhaps she was getting further under his skin than he realized.

After Shelby saw Jed settled into his room, she kissed him and headed for the cardiac wing. After what he had told her about her father's position, she wasn't surprised to find a well-dressed, yet dangerous-looking man seated in front of his room. She smiled and introduced herself to the man. Still, it wasn't until he'd carefully examined her identification that she was allowed inside.

Shelby found her father seated by the window looking out. His navy blue velour robe enveloped a figure that didn't seem quite as large as it had been before. His skin color wasn't as robust as she remembered and he looked frail. Her nose wrinkled at the antiseptic aroma in the room. Even the many bouquets of flowers surrounding them couldn't disguise the smell she always equated with a hospital. She erased the concern from her face and forced a smile to her lips.

"Honestly, I can't leave you alone for a minute without you getting into trouble, can I?" she teased.

Warren Carlisle looked up, his face stiff with shock as he stared at his daughter in disbelief.

"Shelby?" he whispered, as if speaking louder would break the spell. "Is that you?"

"I can't believe it. I don't hear any phones ringing. There are no incoming faxes. No computers spitting out facts and figures." She walked over to her father and dropped a kiss on his forehead. "This must be a red-letter day for the import/export business."

"Oh, baby," he murmured, holding on to her tightly. Tears squeezed out of his eyes as he refused to let go of his daughter. When he finally did, Shelby took a nearby chair and brought it close to his. Warren held her hands as he searched her face. He winced when he saw the scratches and fading bruises on her face and arms.

"I learned the hard way that the great outdoors and I are not compatible," Shelby said lightly. "Now what about you? You haven't lied to the doctors, have you? Are you doing everything they want you to do?"

He grimaced. "I have no choice. No more brandy at bedtime, no more cigars, no more of my favorite foods, and they want me to think about retiring." His expression told her what he thought of the last item.

"From what I understand, you aren't to think about it, you are to do it," she said.

"No one else could handle my job," Warren said fiercely.

"I'm sure there are many qualified people around who could run the office." Shelby spoke carefully.

She sensed it wouldn't be a good idea for her father to find out she knew the truth. Her father a government agent! She still had trouble imagining his carrying a gun or dealing with strange little men in out-of-the-way cafés. Or chasing foreign agents through a city. "The doctor feels you need the rest. Besides, think of all the time you'll have to play golf and perhaps take a vacation," she murmured. "You've always said you wanted to take a cruise up to Alaska. What a perfect time to do it."

"I talked about taking the cruise as a nice break, not because I'd have so much time on my hands I wouldn't know what to do with myself," he grumbled. "Besides, young woman, I want to hear about you. I'm glad Jed was able to get up there and find you."

"Did you doubt he'd succeed?"

"Not at all. He used to spend a lot of time hiking in the mountains," he explained. "I knew if anyone had a chance in finding you, he did. And I didn't have any trust in that sheriff up there."

"Jed did show an affinity for that kind of thing." Shelby wasn't even going to try to trip up her father, no matter how tempting it was. She knew he wouldn't have attained the position he had if he could be so easily caught by an amateur.

Warren squeezed her hands. "I heard there were three men."

"Not in the beginning. Only two broke into Meredith's cabin," she explained. "They decided I'd make a great new playmate for their uncle since the old one was wearing out, and they took me along. The uncle didn't show up for another day. He wasn't my idea of

Mr. Right." She wrinkled her nose. "Luckily, Jed came along that night."

He shook his head. "When I asked him to go up after you, I didn't expect he'd almost get killed in the bargain," he murmured.

"But he didn't. He would have been fine if he hadn't insisted on driving down with me, but I was able to talk him into checking back into the hospital here," she told him. "We left so early this morning that I'm surprised he got any rest today, even if I did do all the driving."

"The man is more stubborn than a Missouri mule." Warren shot his daughter a keen glance. "It sounds as if you two might have settled your differences."

Shelby made a sound of dismissal. "All I have in my bag of tricks is a variety of threats, and I just happened to find the one that worked. I figured if that hadn't worked, I would have brought in the heavy guns. I would have told him I was bringing Meredith over to be his nurse. After several hours in a car with her, I think he would rather climb into a hospital bed and behave himself than spend any more quality time with her."

Warren grimaced. "Good thing. She's all right?"

She nodded. "She plans on dating her doctor."

"She never gives up, does she?" Warren stared at his daughter, noting something new in her eyes, in her manner. He knew her kidnapping would make some changes in her, but he had an idea some of them had been brought about by Jed. Warren dared not hope they had reconciled. At the same time, Jed was his best field agent and he didn't want to lose him. But how could he explain it to her? That he needed someone traveling for him while someone else took over his desk? She must be hoping that man would be Jed, and she'd wonder why he wasn't given the position. Then she would make Warren's life hell until she found out why.

Shelby's shoulders rose and fell in a huge sigh. "I tried calling you I don't know how many times, but all I got was your voice mail," she said in a small voice. "I wanted to tell you I was all right, but I couldn't just leave a message."

He nodded in understanding. "Daniel explained it all to me. I'm afraid he wasn't too sure how my body would take the news. All I know is my heart was glad to hear Jed had found you." He settled back, clearly the man in charge now. "Tell me everything."

Shelby began her story with the night she was rudely awakened by the men breaking into the cabin and didn't stop until she told him how Jed had ended up at the hospital. She thought it best to leave out any intimate details. That was something she preferred to keep to herself.

Warren was stunned at the idea of his little girl picking up a rifle and shooting a man and was gratified that she'd done it. He chuckled when she told him she'd broken the sheriff's nose.

"I had the perfect defense. I was under the influence of a tranquilizer," she explained, which only had him laughing more.

"Pompous fool," he muttered. "I did some checking on him after he gave me a song and dance that they'd do what they could. He's hung on to that position by the skin of his teeth. Something tells me that's going to change very soon.''

''He has a deputy, Rick Howard, who would be perfect for the job,'' she told him.

''Maybe he'll get lucky and take over.''

Shelby had no doubt her father would find a way to make sure Sheriff Rainey was out and Rick was in.

She stared at her father, feeling concern and love welling up inside her. It had been a little over a week since she had last seen him and it was as if he had suddenly turned into an old man.

Concern turned into fear. She had almost lost her father and the man she loved within the space of days. The fear transformed into anger.

''Why did you overwork yourself so badly that you got into this condition?'' she demanded. ''Why couldn't you have slowed down even a year ago? How do you think I would have felt if I'd come back only to learn you'd died because of me?''

Warren opened his arms and she lurched forward. Even in his embrace she could feel a fragility that hadn't been there before. Her well-intentioned vacation had left its mark on all of them.

Chapter 14

Shelby didn't leave her father's room until visiting hours were over and the nurse gently kicked her out. She stopped by Jed's room but found him sound asleep. Since the guard protecting her father was going off duty, he walked her out to Jed's car. During the walk, she learned that his name was Allen and that he'd worked for her father for four years. Even that little bit was like pulling teeth.

"You drive carefully, Miss Carlisle," he suggested. "If you need anything, just call Jasper Thorndyke. Your father has asked him to take over while he's recuperating."

She nodded, familiar with the name although she had never met the man. Now that she thought of it, she realized Jed was one of the very few of her father's employees she'd met over the years. She was tempted to ask if Jasper Thorndyke was also an agent. She had to assume he was.

"All I plan on doing is soaking in the hot tub. Then I'm crawling into bed for a decent night's sleep," she replied, climbing into the car. "Thank you for walking out with me."

His smile was as brief and impersonal as Jed's had been at times. "Just doing my job." He stood there and waited until she started up the car and drove off.

"I can't believe I never noticed any of this before," she murmured, glancing in the rearview mirror and seeing the man's watchful eyes still on her.

By the time Shelby reached her condo, she felt ready to drop. She bypassed the hot tub in favor of a shower, then pulled on a nightgown and dropped into bed. Her head barely felt her pillow before she was sound asleep.

Shelby couldn't remember her alarm clock ever sounding so insistent. Her hand snaked out from under her pillow and slapped at the snooze button, but it didn't stop. She groaned and slid her head out from under her pillow.

"I'm not here," she muttered into the telephone receiver.

"Did you know Bridie has an evil twin down here?" Jed stated without bothering with a greeting. "This one looks like Godzilla."

Shelby's shoulders shook with laughter. "You called me at the crack of dawn just to tell me that?"

"Hell, no! One, it's almost noon, and two, she informed me that I couldn't take a shower this morning, that she would take care of it. The woman is a sadist.''

"Maybe you should compare techniques. She might be able to give you a few tips on dealing with the bad guys,'' she suggested.

"Allen said you stopped by after leaving Warren,'' he said.

"Oh, does Allen report to you, too?''

"Only when I ask him specific questions. Sorry I was asleep when you came by, but the nurse slipped a sleeping pill in with the antibiotic.'' He sounded disgusted.

"I guess they felt you needed the rest.'' She pushed her covers back and sat up, plumping up her pillows behind her. "I can't believe I slept so late.''

"Sounds as if you needed to.''

"Jed, I thought of something. What about that other person—the one you were worried about?'' She thought she shouldn't be too specific. She wondered if knowing the truth about her father and Jed wasn't making her paranoid. "What will happen about him?''

"I've made some calls,'' he replied. "Things will be on hold until I'm released from here.''

"Allen said if I need anything, I'm to call Jasper Thorndyke. I gather he's going to be manning Dad's desk.''

"He's agreed to take over for the time being. Look, we don't need to talk about that. Do you think you can stop by my place and pick up a few things for me?''

"No problem. Just let me get a piece of paper.'' She groped in her bedside table for the pad of paper and pen she kept there. "I plan to come in as soon as I get dressed. Go ahead."

He listed a number of items, then added, "And I need my laptop computer."

"What do you need—"

"Have to go. Godzilla is here to torture me some more." He hung up.

Shelby stared at the phone still in her hand. "Well, goodbye to you, too," she muttered, slamming the phone down. Even if Jed didn't hear her little flash of temper, it made her feel better.

It took Shelby longer than she expected. She'd forgotten she didn't have any food in the house and had to stop for breakfast. As she stepped inside Jed's apartment, she still felt the atmosphere was as sterile as a hotel room. It brought back conflicting emotions, so she was grateful everything he wanted was within easy reach. She tried to ignore the bed as she set a carry-on bag on it. She quickly packed it and left.

"What do you expect to do with your laptop computer?" she demanded, stepping inside his room.

Jed looked more disgruntled than he had the day before. "I have work to do."

"You're supposed to be resting."

"I am resting. I'm sitting in this damn bed, aren't I?" He scowled at her. Even the sight of her wearing a flirty, lemon yellow dress that ended several inches above her knees didn't appear to cheer him up. Although he did seem to perk up when she brushed a light kiss across his lips. "That doesn't mean I can't write up reports that need to be done and update my files. This is as good a time as any to get them done."

Shelby pulled the small computer out of the bag and placed it on his lap, along with several paperback books.

"Since I just knew you'd complain about being bored, I brought you these. Maybe you'll take some time from your all-important work to get in some reading," she told him.

He studied the titles. "One mystery, one horror, one general fiction, one romantic suspense." He cocked an eyebrow at the latter.

"She's an excellent author. You'll love it. It's filled with spies. Besides, variety is good for a person. You make a horrible patient, you know," she informed him. "I've heard the nurses are already drawing lots. The loser gets you. Honestly, can't you behave longer than two seconds?"

"Not when there's work to be done." He lowered his voice. "Don't discuss anything more on the phone, all right?"

She understood his meaning immediately. "I was very careful what I said this morning."

"There is no way you can be careful enough. You haven't learned what can be said and what can't. These lines aren't scrambled and neither is yours. It's just best you don't say anything at all."

Shelby felt stung, as if she had just been scolded like a disobedient child. "I realize I know nothing about your work," she said slowly. "I've come to realize I don't like what you do for a living. I'm not good with secrets. I keep them very well, but I don't like doing it. It was bad enough to find out my father was leading a double life."

"Heart attacks happen to people all the time."

She looked away. "And now I suddenly have to be careful what I say." She turned back to him. "I swear, Jed, I'm beginning to think the worst day in my life was when I met you and the other worst day was when I fell in love with you."

She pushed the carry-on case onto the chair. "There's clothing in here for the day you plan to make your escape."

"Why do you persist in running away?" His question followed her to the door.

Shelby spun around, her skirt flaring around her thighs. "You know, Jed, maybe I'm not running away from something as much as running *to* something," she said softly. "One night of rest and you're raring to get back to your work. Maybe it's because of what you had to leave undone. What will happen when that's taken care of? Something else that will either leave you wounded or killed? Remember what I asked you before? Who will mourn you then?" She walked out of the room.

Jed wanted nothing more than to jump out of bed and run after her. But his wound reopening yesterday had slowed him down more than he wanted to admit. And the new set of stitches hurt like hell.

For a man who always had his life under such strict control, he found himself way out of his depth where Shelby was concerned. He thought of the times he would look at her beautiful face and wonder what it would be like to see that same face for the next fifty years. He already knew she would keep him on his toes that entire time and he would love every minute of it. The word *love* always seemed to come up when he thought of Shelby. The only problem was, did he understand love enough to give her that special gift?

He pounded his fist against the bedcovers.

"A terrorist is easier to deal with than that woman."

Shelby smiled brightly at Allen as she dropped a small stack of magazines in his lap. "There's no reason why you couldn't have some light reading," she told him.

Allen glanced at the titles. All of them had to do with either handguns or mercenaries. The look he gave her was identical to ones she'd gotten from Jed in the past.

"All right, not exactly light reading, but you can keep up with new technology," she said.

"Your friend is already in there," he said.

"Friend?"

He nodded. "She's gorgeous, but she makes a hurricane seem tame."

Shelby could have sworn his eyes looked a little glazed. "Meredith stopped by?"

She walked in to the sound of her father's laughter. Warren sat by the window with Meredith lounging in the chair across from his. Meredith's long legs were encased in a pair of black leather pants that fitted like second skin to her body and a matching vest that bared her arms and midriff.

"Can you breathe in that?" Shelby asked Meredith even as she kissed her father on the cheek.

"Very easily, thank you," she said breezily. "I told Warren the proper way for a man to have a heart attack is during sex, because he can say he was doing something he enjoyed. Then he reminded me the joke usually is the man died that way. I told him he didn't have to go that far." Her lips curved in a broad smile. "Did you notice tall, dark and muscles out there? He's single, not involved with anyone and not gay. He's perfect."

Shelby's head couldn't stop spinning. "What about Dr. Taylor?"

"The man neglected to tell me he had a wife who's been visiting her mother for the past month." She shook her head, clearly not too upset over the loss of a new love. "Can you believe this place?" She waved her hand around. "All this white paint is enough to make you think you're stored inside a refrigerator." She shuddered dramatically. "They should consider getting a better decorator. Just because people are critically ill doesn't mean they can't have some color in their lives."

Warren turned to his daughter. "Meredith tried calling you first, but you'd already left. She thought she'd stop by here with a gift."

That was when Shelby noticed the huge balloon bouquet filling the entire corner of the room. Tiny bells were tied to the multicolored ribbons and tinkled merrily as the balloons drifted back and forth.

"I told him chimes are very soothing to the soul and these are almost as good as the real thing," Meredith explained. "Did you stop by to see Jed?"

She nodded. "He asked that I pick up a few things for him."

"And?" Meredith looked hopeful.

"And he's happily typing away on his laptop computer."

"We talked earlier this morning," Warren said. "He mentioned he was going to call you. He needed to update some files."

"And that's exactly what he's doing," Shelby said much too brightly. "He's got that sucker turned on and he's working away like a busy little bee. I'm sure he'll have his reports whipped out in no time."

"Sarcasm," Meredith confided to Warren. "She's not happy with him." She didn't flinch under Shelby's glare, guaranteed to strip off paint. "All right, I get the hint. But he's still my favorite second father." She got to her feet and leaned over to kiss Warren's cheek.

"Philip was your second father," Shelby reminded her.

"According to my mother he was, but I chose Warren because he has more class." She used the pad of her thumb to rub the bright lipstick off his cheek. "Now you behave yourself with all these nurses running around. I understand there are always scandalous goings-on during the night shift."

"Meredith, I can't imagine anything happening without you around," he said with affection warming his voice.

"Then give me a call, big boy, and I'll be right over," she murmured. "The one I want to hear from is you, Shelby. I want to make sure you're all right. I think I'll see if Warren's guardian angel is free for tonight. He really needs to loosen up."

They could hear her talking to Allen as the door closed after her.

Warren shook his head in wonderment. "I swear being around the woman is like shaking up an open bottle of champagne."

"You ought to visit a Vegas casino with her if you want to find out what fun is like." Shelby smiled, pleased to see more color in her father's face today. She finger-combed his hair, smoothing the thick silver strands. "No matter what happened we were never thrown out."

"Did you see the balloons she brought with her?" he asked. "She said too many flowers makes a person think he's in a funeral parlor and that's the last place I need to think about."

Shelby got up and took a closer look at the helium balloons. "If you can't get any in a hospital, you're dead," she read. Her laughter almost choked in her throat. "That is horrible!"

"That's Meredith."

She nodded. "True." She walked back to her chair and sat down, crossing her legs and carefully arranging her skirt around her knee. "How are you feeling?"

Warren sat back, pressing his palms together in a prayerful attitude. "I'm fine. When are you going to talk about Jed, honey?"

She kept her smile pasted on her face. "May he rot in hell."

"You know you don't mean that. After all, he saved your life."

"And I saved his. We're even."

He heaved a deep sigh. "I'm sorry, Shelby. I was afraid he'd break your heart. I wouldn't have sent him up there, but I couldn't think of anyone better to do the job."

"I realize that, Dad," she said hastily, not wanting him to feel guilty. "It's not that at all. I made the mistake of thinking Jed would be willing to fight for your position since you have to retire. He has no desire to do that. Not even for me." She whispered the last four words. They struck piercing pain in her heart.

He shook his head. "I'll be honest with you. I was surprised the two of you lasted as long as you did. As much as I wanted to talk to you about him, I didn't, since you're an adult and I respect your privacy and Jed's. I could only hope the two of you would find a way to be together or at least part friends."

"I wouldn't say we've parted friends," she said wryly. "Jed doesn't think there's anything wrong between us. I told him it was over weeks ago and he refused to believe me. He felt we just needed to talk things out. The trouble is, any time we talk, we only end up battling. I feel it's better we part and he feels it's better we don't. Except I want a commitment and he can't make one."

"Loners have trouble with that," he murmured.

Shelby fiddled with the catch on her purse. The battle she had been having with herself was finally settled.

"I know what you really do," she said in a low voice.

Warren's head whipped up. "You've known what I do for years," he said with a brief smile.

"I've only known what you've wanted me to know," she corrected. "I saw too much up there in the mountains. A man who's a troubleshooter for an import/export company doesn't have those kind of skills. Even a man who spends time hiking in the mountains doesn't have those kind of skills. I watched Jed cover our tracks so they wouldn't be found. I watched him handle a rifle and a knife as if it was second nature. And I watched him kill a man with that same knife," she said quietly. "I guessed some, he told me some, but he refused to tell me all, so don't be too hard on him. It helped me understand a few things."

Her father looked away, as if unsure what to say. "I should have known I couldn't hide it from you forever. For all of us, it was just a way to do business."

"And it was Jed's life." She was quiet for a moment as she sorted through her thoughts. "Why can't he believe he can have so much more? What would be so wrong for him in staying stateside?"

"He didn't have an easy childhood."

"I know that, too. But that doesn't mean he can't have a full life," she argued.

"You sound as if you're pleading on his behalf," Warren murmured.

Shelby didn't take her eyes off her father's face. "Maybe I am."

"Then I suggest you talk to him about this, not me." He smiled. "Jed loves you a great deal, Shelby. He still might have trouble realizing it, so it's up to you to show him the truth. You've gone through some changes in the last couple of weeks. I'd bet my money on you."

Shelby was afraid to hope. "But he doesn't want it."

"Are you sure?"

"He's said so."

"He also told me he's too old to get shot. I think this last time changed his mind."

Shelby quickly dug through her purse and pulled out perfume, lipstick and blush. She took her time making herself presentable. She dropped everything back inside and studied her father.

"Did Mom ever know?"

He shook his head. "I felt it was safer that way."

"I never thought I could be surprised," Shelby admitted. "I learned very quickly that I could." She kissed him. "If this doesn't work, I'll either be living in sin or brokenhearted for good," she warned him.

He smiled. "I'll take a shotgun after the man if he thinks he's going to live in sin with my daughter."

"That I'd like to see," she quipped.

Shelby fairly flew down the corridor toward the elevator. When she reached Jed's room, she didn't knock but stepped inside. She found him on the telephone, and by the look on his face, he wasn't happy.

"All right, the scrambler is on. What's going on?" His face darkened with anger. "What do you mean you can't find him?" he demanded. "Dammit, all you had to do was keep an eye on him. Was that so difficult?" He showed some surprise at seeing Shelby there but didn't indicate whether he wanted her to stay or go.

She took it as an invitation and sat down in the visitor's chair, shamelessly eavesdropping on his conversation. She heard enough to know what was going on.

"The man you don't trust has disappeared?" she asked when he got off the phone.

He thrust his fingers through his hair, sending the black, shaggy strands falling forward.

"All he had to do was monitor his movements," he muttered. "How difficult could that be? It just goes to show that you can't send someone else to do a job you should have done yourself."

Shelby's heart sank. With a great deal of effort, she forced a smile. "Except you're busy recuperating," she finally managed to say.

"The doctor said if I don't do anything stupid I can be out in a few days."

"Going off after someone who's in better physical shape than you are right now isn't exactly bright," she countered, feeling the tension rise inside her.

Jed paused. "I'm the only one who understands how he thinks."

The silence was deafening.

"And if you get him out of there no one else would have to worry about any damage he can cause," Shelby said slowly.

Jed nodded jerkily. "I have to finish it, Shelby. I can't let someone else do it for me."

She had no idea where her courage came from, but she latched on to it with her fingertips and held on tightly. "Then all I ask is that next time you make sure to duck better than you did the last time," she said huskily.

Jed stilled. "What are you saying?"

She slowly rose to her feet and walked over to the bed, where she carefully sat on the edge. "That you have to do what you do best."

Jed pulled Shelby into his arms and held on as if he was afraid to let go. "What did I ever do to deserve you?" he muttered, feathering kisses across her face.

She smiled. "Wait until you're out of here and we'll discuss that."

Chapter 15

"This is your way of showing me why I deserve you?" Jed teased.

He had been released that afternoon, and Shelby drove him back to her apartment. She had informed him she wanted to pamper him and it was easier for her to do it there. He hadn't the heart to tell her he'd already arranged to leave the next morning. With luck, he could track down Barry and be back with Shelby before she had a chance to miss him.

After a light dinner, she set up the CD player with some sultry jazz and suggested they relax in the hot tub set on the tiny patio just off Shelby's bedroom. Greenery hung down in trailing vines, creating a privacy screen for them.

Jed wasn't certain how Shelby would feel seeing the angry-looking scar, but she only murmured soft words of comfort and kissed the still reddened area.

"I hope the water won't hurt it," she said as they dropped their towels by the hot tub and stepped into the steaming water.

"No, it will be fine," he assured her, unable to keep his eyes off her nude body. All the bruises had disappeared and her cuts had healed. All he saw was lightly tanned skin and deep pink nipples that peaked in the cool air. But there was so much more to her beauty than that. This was the woman who showed him a lighter side of life, and he found himself starting to like it.

"Good." Shelby settled down next to him. She looped her arms around his neck and trailed kisses across his collarbone.

"I thought making love in a hot tub was dangerous to one's health." He groaned when her hand brushed across him.

"Oh, we're not going to make love here," she said in a breathy tone. "We're just going to indulge in some foreplay. Is that all right with you?"

He grasped her by the waist and pulled her up onto his lap. "More than all right." He ran the tip of his tongue across the delicate arch of her eyebrow. He cupped her breast in his palm, feeling the sweet weight. His thumb flicked across the nipple.

Shelby moaned into his open mouth. "I don't want to injure you," she whispered.

"You'll do more injury if you walk away," he said huskily.

She smiled the smile of a siren, meant to seduce. "I don't intend to walk away, Jed. Nor run away."

He grew still as her words sunk in. "Are you sure? I don't know what I can offer you."

She reached down and fondled him, feeling his steely length pulse against her hands. "Then we'll just take it one day at a time."

Jed tasted her with the hunger of a man long denied. It had been an endless long four days in the hospital. Shelby had divided her time between him and her father, and Jed had cherished every moment spent with her. He'd even gritted his teeth when Meredith stopped by with a balloon bouquet—and almost fallen out of bed when he discovered the middle balloon was phallus shaped.

"Just so you don't forget what's important," Meredith explained with a bright smile before drifting off to Warren's room, where she entertained him with cutthroat games of poker.

Jed also learned Allen was falling under the brunette's spell.

"I'm not sure whether to warn him or just let him find out on his own," he told Shelby.

"He's a big boy. He can take care of himself," she'd replied.

At that moment, Jed could not have cared less about anything. Not when he had Shelby in his arms and she wasn't going to run anymore. Now he knew what they meant by something being music to one's ears. He kissed her again and again, thrusting his tongue inside to capture her taste and blend it with his own.

It wasn't long before they realized staying in the hot tub left them in danger of drowning. Shelby climbed out and picked up her towel, wrapping it around her. She knew it wouldn't be a good idea for Jed to try to pick her up.

They ran into the bedroom and fell onto the bed.

"This is much better," Jed murmured, kicking the covers down to the end.

Shelby smiled. "No rocks." Her hands lingered at his waist.

"No dirt everywhere." He nibbled on her earlobe.

"No bugs." She caressed lower.

It took a moment for Jed to think. "No granola bars."

Shelby giggled. "Ah, you ruined tomorrow's breakfast surprise."

Jed pulled her over on top of him. He closed his eyes in bliss as he felt her moist warmth envelop him.

"Now this is what I call physical therapy," he muttered, keeping his hands at her waist as she moved against him in counterpoint to his own rhythm.

Shelby was afraid of breaking open Jed's wound again, and she moved carefully. His eyes remained focused on her face and its variety of emotions. Soon both forgot about his wound as the fire erupted within them.

Afterward, they lay on their sides, their legs tangled together. Jed stroked Shelby's hair away from her face where damp strands had clung to her cheeks and lips. Lips he couldn't resist kissing again and again.

"I understand the nurses threw a party when they found out you were being discharged." Shelby traced the line of his collarbone.

"There were a few who mourned my departure," he teased.

"Maybe that's what they told you...."

Jed kissed the words away. Then he abruptly yawned. "Sorry."

"You still need to rest," she reminded him, as she reached down for the covers and pulled them up over their bodies.

Jed thought of telling her he was leaving in the morning, then discarded the idea. This time, he didn't want anything to mar their time together. It wasn't long before he felt her body slacken as she drifted off to sleep.

"I guess they were right," he murmured against her hair. "You accomplished the impossible, Shelby. I fell in love with you."

Shelby wasn't alarmed when she woke up late that morning and found Jed gone. Until she realized the shower wasn't running and the rooms felt too quiet.

"Jed?" she called out.

What if something's happened to him and he can't answer?

Alarmed, she jumped out of bed and made a quick survey of the condo. It wasn't until she reached the entryway that she found the envelope with her name written in a bold hand on the front.

"No," she whimpered. Her hand trembled as she reached for the envelope and tore it open.

I know. You're furious with me for not telling you ahead of time, but I thought it would be better this way. I need to be the one to settle the problem. I hope you still understand that.

You weren't the only one rescued up that mountain. You rescued a part of me, too.

Love,
Jed

Shelby's eyes sparkled with tears as she traced the word *love*.

"I knew there was hope for you," she whispered.

"And you're absolutely sure you're doing the right thing?" Meredith asked Shelby over the phone.

Shelby held the cordless unit between her ear and shoulder as she leaned toward the bathroom mirror and applied mascara.

"Oh, yes."

"Are you going to the airport?"

"Dad was able to find out what time he'd be coming in so I could meet the plane," she replied. "Jed had hoped to be gone less than a week and instead was gone three weeks. I'm not about to let him walk off that plane and not see me."

"Then I'm very glad for you."

"How's it going with Allen?"

"The man is so stoic it's incredible. I told him if I didn't know better I'd swear he worked for the government," Meredith exclaimed.

Shelby choked on her laughter. "Really?"

"Are you all right?"

"Fine," she said in a high-pitched voice.

"Allen told me I have an incredible imagination and I told him I didn't care what he did."

Shelby glanced at her watch. "Meredith, I have to run if I want to be there in time."

"Yes, you have three weeks to make up for." She chuckled. "Have fun!"

Shelby drove to the airport with one eye watching the rearview mirror. The last thing she needed was a speeding ticket. The day before, she had seen her father off on a cruise to Alaska. Judging from the interested looks he had gotten from several women, she doubted he'd lack for company.

Shelby already had the proper paperwork to allow her into the private terminal where Jed's plane would land. She made sure to arrive early and eagerly paced the length of the small building.

"Miss Carlisle," the dispatcher called out. "Mr. Hawkins's flight is landing now."

She ran to the double doors and pushed them outward. She was standing at the top of the steps when the private jet rolled to a stop and the door slid open. She stood on tiptoes, ready with a cheery wave, when Jed appeared in the open doorway. The first thing she noticed was that he was in need of a shave, his clothes were rumpled and he looked tired.

Shelby's smile dimmed further when he descended the metal stairway with a decided limp, carrying a cane in one hand.

Even the look of astonishment on his face and the warmth flooding his features as he slowly made his way toward her couldn't bring back her smile.

"What happened?" she demanded, bracing her hands on her hips. "Did you get shot again? I swear, Jed Hawkins, you're looking to get killed! What am I going to have to do? Tie you to the bed to keep you safe?" She was shouting by the time he hauled her into his arms and silenced her the best way he knew.

As always, Shelby melted under his kiss. But it didn't stop the picture of him limping toward her.

"Yes, I had a pleasant flight and yes, our traitor is now in custody." He deliberately answered questions she hadn't asked. "And no, I didn't get shot."

She punched him in the shoulder. "You shouldn't have frightened me that way! Then what happened? He didn't use a knife, did he? Or something else?"

Jed grimaced. He draped an arm around her shoulders as they walked into the terminal.

"Nothing that dramatic. I was running for my flight and I slid on a wet patch on the floor and sprained my ankle," he groused. He tightened his grip and stopped Shelby midstep. "I have to tell you, I'm too damn old for all this. Jasper wants to return to his old office and I told him I'd be willing to take over Warren's."

Shelby's breath caught in her throat. "Not because of me," she whispered.

He shook his head. His eyes were warm with the love Shelby wanted from him.

"No, this last assignment showed me it's time to slow down. I only took this one because it was personal. Barry had been a part of my team and I wanted to be the one to bring him in," he admitted, turning her around so they could continue walking. "So when are you going to marry me?"

Shelby's steps faltered. "Marry?"

"Sure. You're not going to keep leading me on, are you? After all, we've been seeing each other for quite some time now. The next logical step is marriage."

She shook her head to clear it. "What happened to the Jed Hawkins who didn't believe in commitment?"

He grinned. "He got smart." Just as quickly his grin disappeared. "And more important, I don't want to lose you." He drew her into his arms. "I knew it when I was going after you up that mountain. I just had to convince myself more. Luckily, you did a better job of convincing me.''

"You won't miss the field work?'' She was too afraid she was dreaming.

"I won't miss people shooting at me,'' he replied. "It's time, Shel. Time for me to make that next step. All I'm asking is that you make it with me.''

"*Yes!*'' she squealed, launching herself into his arms and almost unbalancing him as she kissed him.

"Just one thing,'' Jed gasped when they broke apart. "You don't go off without me anymore. I don't want to have to climb any more mountains after you.''

Shelby couldn't stop smiling. "No more Mister Nice Guy?'' she teased, reminding him of a retort he'd made during their escape.

"Oh, sweetheart, from now on I intend to be the nicest guy around,'' he said huskily, covering her mouth with his again.

"Something tells me that won't be too difficult for you to do,'' she murmured.

* * * * *

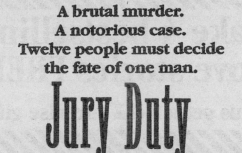

Take 4 bestselling love stories FREE

Plus get a FREE surprise gift!

Special Limited-time Offer

Mail to Silhouette Reader Service™

3010 Walden Avenue
P.O. Box 1867
Buffalo, N.Y. 14240-1867

YES! Please send me 4 free Silhouette Intimate Moments® novels and my free surprise gift. Then send me 6 brand-new novels every month, which I will receive months before they appear in bookstores. Bill me at the low price of $3.34 each plus 25¢ delivery and applicable sales tax, if any.* That's the complete price and a savings of over 10% off the cover prices—quite a bargain! I understand that accepting the books and gift places me under no obligation ever to buy any books. I can always return a shipment and cancel at any time. Even if I never buy another book from Silhouette, the 4 free books and the surprise gift are mine to keep forever.

245 BPA A3UW

Name	(PLEASE PRINT)	
Address		Apt. No.
City	State	Zip

This offer is limited to one order per household and not valid to present Silhouette Intimate Moments® subscribers. *Terms and prices are subject to change without notice.
Sales tax applicable in N.Y.

UMOM-696   ©1990 Harlequin Enterprises Limited

As seen on TV!
Free Gift Offer

With a Free Gift proof-of-purchase from any Silhouette® book, you can receive a beautiful cubic zirconia pendant.

This gorgeous marquise-shaped stone is a genuine cubic zirconia—accented by an 18" gold tone necklace.

(Approximate retail value $19.95)

Send for yours today...
compliments of *Silhouette*®

To receive your free gift, a cubic zirconia pendant, send us one original proof-of-purchase, photocopies not accepted, from the back of any Silhouette Romance™, Silhouette Desire®, Silhouette Special Edition®, Silhouette Intimate Moments® or Silhouette Yours Truly™ title available in August, September or October at your favorite retail outlet, together with the Free Gift Certificate, plus a check or money order for $1.65 U.S./$2.15 CAN. (do not send cash) to cover postage and handling, payable to Silhouette Free Gift Offer. We will send you the specified gift. Allow 6 to 8 weeks for delivery. Offer good until October 31, 1996 or while quantities last. Offer valid in the U.S. and Canada only.

Free Gift Certificate

Name: _____

Address: _____

City: _____ State/Province: _____ Zip/Postal Code: _____

Mail this certificate, one proof-of-purchase and a check or money order for postage and handling to: SILHOUETTE FREE GIFT OFFER 1996. In the U.S.: 3010 Walden Avenue, P.O. Box 9077, Buffalo NY 14269-9077. In Canada: P.O. Box 613, Fort Erie, Ontario L2Z 5X3.

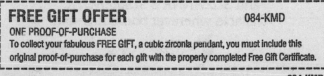

FREE GIFT OFFER   084-KMD

ONE PROOF-OF-PURCHASE

To collect your fabulous FREE GIFT, a cubic zirconia pendant, you must include this original proof-of-purchase for each gift with the properly completed Free Gift Certificate.

084-KMD

There's nothing quite like a family

REUNION

HANNAH · MICHAEL · KATE

The new miniseries by
Pat Warren

Three siblings are about to be reunited.
And each finds love along the way....

HANNAH
Her life is about to change now that she's met
the irresistible Joel Merrick in HOME FOR HANNAH
(Special Edition #1048, August 1996).

MICHAEL
He's been on his own all his life. Now he's
going to take a risk on love...and
take part in the reunion he's been
waiting for in MICHAEL'S HOUSE
(Intimate Moments #737, September 1996).

KATE
A job as a nanny leads her to Aaron Carver,
his adorable baby daughter and the
fulfillment of her dreams in KEEPING KATE
(Special Edition #1060, October 1996).

Meet these three siblings from

Silhouette SPECIAL EDITION®
and
INTIMATE MOMENTS®
™ *Silhouette*

Look us up on-line at: http://www.romance.net

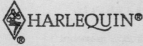